A Poetess and an Heir

Ann Hawthorne

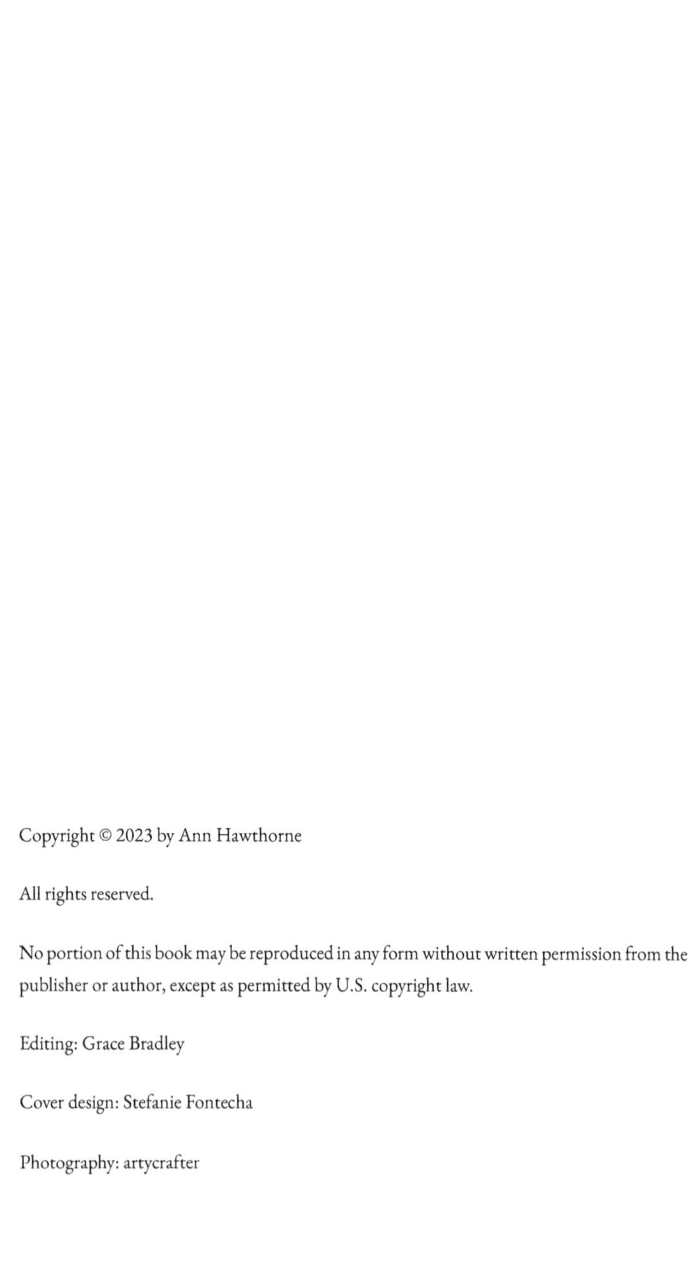

Contents

Chapter 1

F elicity Deacon hadn't seen the inside of Morwood Hall for almost ten years. As far as her hostess was concerned, she has never seen it all, and Felicity thought this blissful ignorance should be allowed to live on.

Although her memories were partly blurred by the inevitable passing of years, and partly suppressed with her considerable force of will, Felicity still couldn't help but notice the changes. The dark, thick Aubusson carpets that had once smothered the floors had been replaced by lighter Axminster ones. Either Mr. Winters started to interest himself in the niceties of fashion in the last years of his life, or, more likely, his second wife had.

Most of the withdrawing room, however, remained the same as Felicity remembered—a touch more grandiose than such a place for intimate gatherings strictly required to be, luxurious as thick cream, with brocatelle curtains framing the windows.

Mrs. Abigail Winters, surprisingly young, smiled benevolently as she had probably noticed her guest's curiosity. A guest was a rather generous word, however—whatever courtesies were preserved, no one could pretend that Felicity was on anything like an equal footing with the dainty Mrs. Winters. The former might have been the veritable toast of London's literary gatherings, and the latter a widow of a trade-wealthy squire whose name was hardly known outside Somerset, but it mattered not. One had to earn her living, however genteel the profession; the other did not.

'I am so glad you have accepted my invitation, Miss Deacon', Abigail said, pouring them both a cup of pekoe—flowery orange, of course, the highest grade. 'Summer in the country can be so very dreadfully boring. When my dear husband was still with us, we used to mostly live in town. His matters of business demanded it, of course. Edmund had free run of Morwood Hall'.

'I imagine that has changed, now that your stepson is a man grown and likely to be in want of a wife'. Felicity's memories of Edmund Winters, the playmate of her childhood games who she had once considered to be her twin soul created for her by the Almighty himself, were rather better than those of his house. She recalled the stubborn gray eyes, the dark hair soft under her fingers as she teased him over this joke or other, the lanky limbs.

He had never been the kind of ravishing creature who would set any novel-reading lady's heart aflutter. This she could judge now with the ruthlessness and experience of years. Nonetheless, she could imagine he would not lack for invitations by these ladies' rather more level-headed mothers. His name might be young and green, and his family's possession of Morwood Hall anything but ancestral, but the prospective of having a son-in-law who actually can pay the tradesmen's bills must be enticing indeed at least to some.

This, too, Felicity could judge with experience.

'Oh, Edmund would not hear of that', Mrs. Winters suddenly replied. 'One would never find a young man less interested in the delights of the town, or in anything to do with the marriage mart, than him. To hear my stepson, he would be perfectly happy conversing with trees, brooks, and tenants.'

Had the circumstances been different, Felicity would have bristled at the fact that all these entities were evidently perceived by Mrs. Winters to be of the same order. She would have had to keep that response under control, in the grim confines of her head, but she would have bristled nonetheless.

As it was, however, she had to put her cup back very, very carefully, for the fear of spilling the contents on the carpet—such was the shiver that ran through her.

'Do you mean that Mr. Winters is here?' Felicity asked, hoping her voice was as steady and courtly as she had trained it to be when dealing with influential patrons.

'Why, yes. Pray do not worry, Miss Deacon, he is unlikely to be a nuisance. He has little interest in poetry and even less interest in human company."

Felicity could only bear to answer something so noncommittal that it didn't even touch her mind on the way to her lips.

Edmund Winters was here, on this estate. Perhaps, in this very house. What was he going to think when he saw her—which he would inevitably do one day, if in passing, if from afar? Was he going to even remember her? Or, if he would, was he going to look upon her with pity? Once the daughter of an ambitious father, a neighbor, someone striving to be an equal, now a supplicant before a patron?

Perhaps, she reflected, she made a mistake when she accepted the sudden invitation. But she had been so sure that a young man of considerable fortune would never choose to spend the summer in the country. Besides, she was so desperate...

On the other hand, Edmund Winters had never been the sort of gentleman one imagined upon hearing about a young man of considerable fortune. Even as a child, even as a youth, he had always been rather solitary, fond of strenuous exercise, and proud to the point of sullenness.

Solitary, that is, with one exception. That exception had been the neighbor's daughter, the girl with unruly dark curls and the kind of energy that could not be satisfied by running with hoops to improve her figure (which her mother insisted she do).

But that had been a long time away, Felicity reminded herself. A great gulf of years separated her from that girl with her innocent wildness. For all she knew, he was a veritable rake now, perhaps, or at the very least a man-about-town.

'The Lavender Cottage had been prepared for you, Miss Deacon', Mrs. Winters mentioned. 'It's a trifle far from the house proper, that is true, but...'

Felicity put on a smile that felt like a counterfeit porcelain even before Mrs. Winters finished speaking. She was grateful for a small cottage on the premises, of course—ever, ever so grateful! She, who had once taken tea with this woman's rather more stern predecessor countless times, who had ridden dappled horses with the estate's heir, was now grateful to be housed in the Lavender Cottage safely far from the stately home itself.

She did not get a chance to utter the supposed gratitude in question, however—any more than Mrs. Winters herself got a chance to finish her phrase. For, at that moment, the door to the withdrawing room opened abruptly, and a tall young man strode in. Although he was dressed with stern impeccability, he had the ruffled air of someone who had just come back from a bout of riding.

'Mrs. Winters', he addressed the older woman. 'We need to speak of...'

Abigail Winters coughed with the utmost delicacy.

'Edmund, we have a guest'.

At this, Edmund Winters—for, of course, it could be no one else—turned, and looked Felicity in the eye.

She stared back.

He had changed, that much was true. Although he still was no perfect beau of Viscountess Granville's novels, the last years had been kind to him. The uncomfortably lanky limbs were no longer so; rather, he was slim in the way that hinted that his horse-riding expeditions must have been rather frequent.

The gray eyes were stubborn still, but Felicity could not recall them having ever been so light, so piercing.

'Edmund', she called out without thinking. The years fell away for a second, as did the notions of what was prope–r—and the knowledge that calling a man who was so infinitely above her now by his Christian name was most certainly not on that list.

His eyes widened in a barely perceptible way.

'Felicity'. His voice was just as soft as hers. If one didn't see her, but judged the proceedings solely upon his expression, one would have thought he saw the headless ghost of Anne Boleyn walking the corridors of the Tower, not a pink-satin-clad living woman in a sunlit withdrawing room.

Although, perhaps, the latter really was a more dire vision. Or, at least, a more personal one. Edmund Winters hadn't, after all, cut Anne Boleyn's head off himself.

The thought helped Felicity regain the hold over herself.

'Miss Deacon,' she corrected him in the tone she always used with her betters when she didn't want them to know they were being corrected.

'Miss Deacon. To what do I owe this pleasure?' His bearings returned, too, that much was clear. The self-control, which she used to compare to a particularly well-starched collar, was in place once again.

'To my invitation, of course', Mrs. Winters chimed in. 'Why, Edmund, do you not recall it?'

'No, Mother, I do not'.

He called his stepmother Mother, no doubt to mollify her feelings. Correct as always.

'I am positively sure I have discussed it with you', Abigail Winters insisted. 'Did I not tell you that the ennui in summer is dreadful?'

'Yes, Mother. That, I do remember. Indeed, we have had conversations on the subject of your ennui so often the notion had imprinted itself on my mind like a pamphlet'.

'How peculiar. I was sure I have told you that I decided to deal with that inconvenience by engaging in some patronage of the arts'.

'So you have, but I rather thought you were going to commission Mr. Lawrence for another portrait, not invite guests'.

'Miss Deacon is going to stay in the Lavender Cottage. Do not worry, Edmund, she is not going to interrupt your vital business'.

'I hadn't thought you were such an ardent admirer of Miss Deacon's poetry,' Edmund Winters said quietly. There was suspicion in his voice, and a mere trace of hurt, like a smudge of red paint.

Felicity was a poet, first and foremost. She knew how to recognize the shades of feelings in the supposedly proper men and women around her, just as she knew the names for different shades of flowers.

In those last years, she had mostly seen the flowers in question upon botanical drawings, but that was no matter at all.

'I did not even know you knew her name, Edmund', Abigail Winters retorted. 'Have you yourself been one of those ardent admirers while at Cambridge? I know that students used to run riot over her first poems, when she still published as The Merry One'.

'I did not even know The Merry One was a lady', Mr. Winters replied. 'Much less that it had been one I once knew'.

Felicity knew she shouldn't have been wounded by these word–s—after all, Edmund Winters has never been the sort of man to agonize over the hidden meanings of poetic lines in the best of times. Besides, even if he were, it was sheer folly to imagine that he would somehow deduce the identity of the young woman he hadn't seen since her girlhood merely by the manner of her versifying.

But wounded she was.

'You knew each other?' Abigail Winters exclaimed with genuine-looking amazement, therefore clearing herself of suspicion. 'But how?'

This time, Felicity could reply for herself.

'My father used to rent a rather splendid house not far from here. I had the honor of calling upon Mr. Winters once in a while'.

'My goodness, but if your situation had been so comfortable, what on earth led you to earning your own living by the quill?'

Felicity shuddered inwardly. The second Mrs. Winters was not a malicious woman by any stretch of the imagination, but she clearly didn't suffer from the surfeit of tact.

She did not lower her gaze, but looked into the young widow's cloudless blue eyes.

'The American War has ruined more than one livelihood, Mrs. Winters. That country house was the least of the things we had to let go of'.

And the vultures were waiting by the door.

'I did not know of your...circumstances', Edmund Winters said, looking at Felicity. Such precise choice of words. Circumstances. Another man might have said ruin, but no such dramatic expressions in the measured world of Morwood Hall.

The old Mr. Winters had been the same, as far as Felicity could remember. The son did grow up to follow his father.

But then, she should have guessed that.

'It was not your responsibility to do anything, Mr. Winters.' Felicity smiled with as much formal charm as she could muste-r—and she could muster considerable resources on that front. 'It is not, after all, as though I had been your intended'.

Edmund could not help staring at the closed door for a few moments after Felicity Deacon had been escorted out of the room. She was accompanied by a footman who had been told to show her to her new accommodation. Edmund wondered if it was courtesy on his stepmother's part, or ignorance. She had rarely taken any interest in the parts of the estate beyond Morwood Hall proper, and might have simply not known where Lavender Cottage was located.

God, what a predicament it all was.

'I hope you understand, Mother', he turned to Mrs. Winters, his words clipped and clear, 'that Miss Deacon cannot stay with us for long'.

'I hope you understand that I cannot go back on my promise. I have promised her the run of the cottage for the rest of the summer, and that is what she is going to get'.

'The rest of the summer. Which has barely started'.

'Indeed. May I ask why you object to her presence so? Did she not say you used to know each other? Even if some childhood rivalry lies between you, I do hope you can set it aside, being a man grown'.

Childhood rivalry. He could have laughed at it, had he been in any mood for laughter. No, there was no rivalry, no juvenile enmity. If anything, there was an enchantment.

But Edmund had made his choice, all those years ago, in his father's study. He realized, even then, that enchantments were for children, and games in the meadows. A man had to make difficult choices, and, if need be, drink the bitter drought to the dregs.

'I cannot imagine Miss Cadogan would see it quite this way', Edmund said aloud instead. 'To say nothing of Sir Jonathan'.

'It is not as though Miss Deacon would live under the same roof as yourself."His stepmother waved the objection away, as though it were but an annoying fly. 'I cannot say anything for Sir Jonathan's daughter, but he himself is a reasonable man'.

'He might suspect my relationship with Miss Deacon to be improper'.

'He is no sermon-writer himself, from what I hear'.

'But not when it comes to his daughter. In that case, he would demand the behavior of her suitor to be one of the utmost correctness. Quite rightly, of course'.

Edmund could hardly imagine having a daughter of a marriageable age, but he supposed that if he had one, he would have never allowed a man of rakish habits to court her. Especially, his pragmatic side added, if those habits were coupled with a recent possession of the land, and the fact that he was a mere generation away from trade.

It was not difficult to imagine how Priscilla Cadogan might develop some suspicions of her own. Not that she herself was not lovely—the color of her hands was that of placid pallor, and her fair hair might have belonged to a Meissen shepherdess. However, she lacked that unnameable quality that animated Miss Deacon's veins even when she was but a sprightly girl. Edmund could remember Felicity Deacon reading Homer in his father's gleaming-new, mostly untouched library, and pronouncing she would not want to die through any way but a shipwreck.

She has changed with years, as he supposed most women change when they grow and mould themselves to the necessary demands of the world. There was a hint of polish in her deportment, and the kind of self-control in her voice that had not been there before. But she still had that dark hair curling of its own accord, those eyes so deeply brown they could almost be twin black ponds.

The expression he saw when he looked into those eyes for the first time in years could not be mistaken for anything but shock. Even that was bright and intense in her, a primary color.

'Miss Deacon is my guest, in a certain way. She would expect my behavior as a hostess to be one of the utmost correctness, too. I have offered her our hospitality, and our hospitality she is going to have. Of course', Mrs. Winters added, 'you can remind me that I am merely a widow, and not your true mother; that it is only through your good favor that I am not residing in one of those cottages myself...'

Edmund furrowed his brow in mild irritation. This was a crude instrument to employ on her part.

Which was not to say it was ineffective.

'You know very well that I would never wrong you. I have never expressed the faintest desire to turn you out of father's house, and I never will. This is your home as well as mine...Mother'.

She smiled as though she were a soft white cat having come upon a dish of soft white cream.

'In that case, since it is my home as well as yours, I am sure you won't begrudge me my choice of guests'.

God, what a predicament it was.

'I am going to join Sir Jonathan's hunting party tomorrow', Edmund reminded her. 'I dearly hope he is not going to ask me why a woman of uncommon beauty is currently residing on my estate just as I am trying to court his daughter. In your place, I would harbor the same hope'.

'You know my opinion on Sir Jonathan Cadogan and his daughter very well'.

'I do, and I cannot understand it'.

'Such caricatures of snobbery as they could have been drawn by Hogarth'.

'They have the right to it. The Cadogans' claim to their land stems from the days King Henry dissolved the monasteries. No lineage in this corner of Somerset is more proud'.

'Proud is the right word'.

'More proud, or more worthy of joining our own to. Father had always held this opinion'.

'Edmund, my dear, even I did not always agree with your father's opinions, and I was his wife sworn to honor him. I see no reason why you should'.

'That', Edmund smiled, 'is because the responsibility for our family's wellbeing is not yours. It is mine'.

Even as he spoke these words, however, a thought of Felicity Deacon flared up in his mind. Like his stepmother, she had no man in the family; she was not even a woman back when she first took quill in her hands, but a slip of a girl. However, if she told them the whole stor–y—and what was there to omit?—she took it upon herself to restore and promote her family's comfort with no brother, husband, and, in short time, no father either to support her.

Whatever his opinions on the correct way of doing things, he could not help but respect such resilience.

Chapter 2

F elicity found she rather liked the Lavender Cottage. Despite the modest name, it was clearly not the residence of a gamekeeper or anyone of a similar kind. This creation of brick and gray stucco had clearly been made for someone used to comfort—at least, in the older definition of comfort that had prevailed in the days of the first Georges. No Axminster carpets here, of course, but the small parlor had an oil cloth on the floor, and the bedroom upstairs had a fine view of the willows.

Felicity supposed that the correct thing to do would have been to wait for one of Mrs. Winters' maids to come and help her unpack. However, the days when she was used to servants at her beck and call were long since past, and in the intervening years she had developed the kind of easy self-sufficiency that grows quickly in youth if not stifled. Therefore, now, she opened one of the sash windows to let some of the fresh air in, and started to extract her possessions from the trunks.

They were not that numerous, so she had almost finished by the time she heard a knock upon the door.

Felicity paused before opening it. Living in the city had taught her caution. For all that, back home, she still lodged with her mother for the sake of respectability, they were just two women in a violent stormy sea that was London, and couldn't offer much defense in case dark trouble came upon their doorstep.

But, Felicity reminded herself, here, she was in the green heart of a prosperous estate that was Morwood Hall. These rolling acres were not exactly crawling with ruffians.

Nonetheless, she tiptoed over to the window and glanced out of it to get a glimpse of her visitor. Just in case.

The sight awarded her some relief, but sharpened discomfort of a different kind.

'I see you have found the Lavender Cottage to be comfortable', Edmund Winters said, stiff-necked as always, as he looked beyond her shoulder into the room.

'I would have been a very spoiled young woman indeed not to have found it so'.

Felicity could have told herself she did not intend these words as a pinprick to the pride of the man who had once been her twin soul, but she was not in the habit of lying to herself.

'You have never been spoiled, Miss Deacon. Not even when your family lived in great comfort'. He smiled—slightly, formally, but smiled nonetheless. It was as if the sunlight outside had finally touched his face, for all that he was standing with his back to the light of the day.

'I would have invited you inside and offered you refreshments, but I am afraid I am yet to explore the kitchen'.

'You wouldn't have to find your way around the kitchen yourself, of course...'

'No? Who is going to do that for my sake, then? Elfin creatures from the woods?' Felicity laughed at the last moment to ameliorate the tartness of the comment, remembering—not without some pain—that she was speaking not to her friend or even a former friend now, but to her superior. Her patron. Her *better*.

'Has Mother not sent a maid to help you?'

'Not as far as I can see. I thought she was intending to do that later'.

'Perhaps that is true. But I am going to remind her nonetheless'.

'I would be grateful if you do, Mr. Winters'.

It should have rankled more, this unspoken almost-confirmation that Abigail Winters hasn't given a thought to how exactly her pet poetess was going to live in the cottage that was never meant for solitary habitation and solitary housekeeping. His stepmother had dashed a letter of invitation off, ameliorated her boredom, and gave no more thought to the boring living arrangements this would necessitate than a child would about the nourishment of her doll.

By now, however, Felicity was rather used to the thoughtless ways of those above her, and, against the backdrop of some monstrosities she had lived through, this seemed so small as to be almost charming.

'It was... I did not expect to see you again', Edmund told her after a pause.

'Ever again in your life? England is not so large a country as this, surely, and the *ton* is a veritable village'.

'I would hardly know, Miss Deacon. I have always shunned it'.

'Always?'

'Since I was old enough to have a choice'.

'I... I do remember that', Felicity replied quietly. 'You have ever been a lonely child'.

'Not as lonely as you were'.

'I had my mother'. Her father had been alive back then, too, of course; but business took him to the capital often enough that his presence was rare as snowfall in July.

'I remember your mother well. A most...pragmatic woman'.

The smile Felicity gave him was even more strained than his own. Pragmatic was one word. It was plain Edmund Winters wanted to say a rather different one, but Felicity knew he would rather allow himself to be torn apart by his own hunting dogs than hurl an insult at a vulnerable woman.

Correct in every way, as always.

Deep down, she wished he had not been so. She wished he could give words and flesh to the impulses that were raging in her own mind, that he gave her a fire of indignation she could merrily stoke.

But he did not. He could not. He simply continued staring at her, politely, relentlessly.

What have you done to us?

'That she was', Felicity responded noncommittally, her words bland as gray fish. 'That she still is, of course'.

An uncomfortable silence stretched between them, congealing.

'Well.' Edmund coughed. 'I would go back and remind Mother about the matter of your maid'.

'Thank you. I am most grateful'.

Felicity did not close the door immediately when her visitor turned his back. On the contrary, she stood on the doorstop for a long while, blind to the flowers and deaf to the birdsong, and watched the figure of Edmund Winters disappear down the bend of the path until she could not see him anymore, but could only see the green stillness of the garden.

Mr. Winters kept his promise, and a pretty young woman by the name of Rose turned up upon the doorstep of the cottage the evening of the same day. The maid was clearly curious about the dark and merry London poetess she was to attend to for the whole summer, and Felicity played the part. She even declaimed one of the short poems from her early days as resident poet for the *Fine-Letters Gazette*, much to Rose's delight.

'Oh, Miss Deacon', she exclaimed, 'to think you probably read this to duchesses!'

Felicity's first impulse was to deny that, to tell her that her verses were anything but a gilded exclusive thing. But then she changed her mind. It clearly gave the girl pleasure to think she was given something hitherto available only to grand noble patronesses, and who was Felicity to deny her pleasure?

Instead of doing such a nonsensical and frankly cruel thing, Felicity questioned her carefully about the plans of the inhabitants of Morwood Hall.

'It's no great plans." Rose shrugged. 'Mr. Winters is going away to Sir Jonathan Cadogan's house for a week, I think. They're going to hunt hares or some such'.

Felicity breathed out a sigh of relief. The less time she had to spend with Edmund Winters, the better. She had an idea that necessitated her asking something of his stepmother. For all her gratitude for Rose's presence, she didn't want to risk running into him again and suffering another strained attempt at polite conversation.

'But if you ask me', the maid continued, 'he's going there to hunt a very different sort of prey'.

'What do you mean?'

'Sir Jonathan's daughter. She'd make a fine bride for Mr. Winters, everyone's saying. I've not been here in those days, but the housekeeper says even Mr. Winters' father, God rest his soul, was talking about something of that sort'.

'With Sir Jonathan?'

For two men to arrange a marriage between their children sounded decidedly old-fashioned, but Felicity wouldn't have put it past the late Mr. Winters the elder. Not that she had discerned any genuine love for traditions in him back when she knew him, but no one could outdo him in sheer opportunism.

Felicity knew, of course, the convention that claimed it ill to speak badly of the dead. She didn't, however, speak of this particular dead at all right now. The adage prescribed nothing against thinking.

'No, Miss Deacon. With his son. With the young Mr. Winters, that is. I've heard they've had an almighty row, but the young Mr. Winters gave way in the end'.

'Does he speak often of it? The young Mr. Winters, that is?' The clarification was unneeded, stupid, even—as though the dead could speak!

On the other hand, the dead could influence the affairs of the living; could stretch their pale hands from out of the grave and choke the life out of people with beating hearts. So why not speak, too, if through other mouths?

'With his stepmother. That is, it's not as if there's anyone else for a fine gentleman like him to talk to, round here. It's Priscilla Cadogan whom he wants to hunt. That is, to court'.

Felicity had heard the name, of course. She had heard it even in her childhood, when she could pretend that Edmund—the young Mr. Winters—and she were equals in their wilderness, and could both laugh at their betters behind closed doors. Now that she strained her memory a little, she was sure she could even recall glimpsing Priscilla Cadogan once or twice during the outings to Bath. The memory was slight, something trembling on the edge of her mind. A soft figure sitting still in a sedan chair.

A fine bride for Mr. Winters. But then, why wouldn't she be? He had grown up, after all, just as Felicity had. He had learned not to laugh at his betters instead of soliciting their benevolence. Not even behind closed doors.

'Thank you, Rose', Felicity said, her smile beaming like fool's gold. 'It's astonishing, really, how much you know!'

She didn't quite understand, why was it that the notion of Edmund Winters courting this pretty girl seems so... Not exactly abhorrent, but somehow unnatural. That was the way of the world. He was an heir to a great fortune, and she was a lady of a fine and noble name. Nor did she, Felicity, know anything incriminating about Priscilla Cadogan. And even if she did, the personal happiness of Edmund Winters was not her concern. After all, her own happiness, or even her own safety, ceased to be his concern a great while ago.

Nonetheless, she waited a few days until he was, according to Rose, away on the hunting trip, before she went after Morwood Hall to call upon Mrs. Winters.

Mrs. Winters looked at her with astonishment when Felicity voiced her request.

"A journal?" asked the young widow. "But what on earth do you need a journal for?"

"To write down my observations of various nature, of course." Felicity smiled. "I find that Somerset is so beautiful in summer—even more beautiful than I remember it to be. I thought, perhaps some imagery might inspire me".

Strangely enough, that was the exact truth of the situation. Felicity had not told this part to Mrs. Winters, and was unlikely to ever tell her the whole truth now, but her acceptance of the invitation had as much to do with her state as it did with her ambitions. Indeed, if it were not for the state in question, she might have well remained in London. She always found herself loath to leave the fashionable circles that provided her with livelihood. After all, the memory of the *ton* was always short indeed.

But she had driven herself too much, too fast. Had she been a horse, her sides would have been covered with bloody foam. She told herself sternly many times that it was her own choice, that no one was at fault for Felicity Deacon's misfortunes but Felicity Deacon herself. However, it didn't mollify her mind, nor did it bring rest to her body.

This sojourn in Somerset, Felicity decided when she'd held Mrs. Winters' letter in her hand, was to be her rest and recuperation—her convalescence, in a way. Perhaps, by the end of the summer, she would be well enough to start her writing routine anew, to produce the steady stream of heartfelt poems that Mr. Flyte demanded of her.

No, she corrected herself, as though someone could have heard her even in the privacy of her mind. He didn't demand it of her. The public demanded it of her. Life itself demanded it of her. The world had. And if the world was a greatly unfair place, it was not Mr. Flyte's fault, and not her mother's fault.

"I am not quite a journal keeper, Miss Deacon." Mrs. Winters shrugged. "But I'm sure the widow Kerr in her shop might have some".

"In her shop?" Felicity asked.

It would have been hyperbole to say she was incredulous at the mention, but she was certainly quite surprised. The village of her childhood had no shop to speak of, any more than it had a circulating library. News and goods from the outside world arrived in the sacks of the peddlers, especially those who plied local fairs.

Mrs. Winters has clearly noticed her surprise, for her eyes lit up at this topic as they never did at the notion of keeping a journal.

"Oh, yes," she nodded. "It is another recent development, to be sure, but my husband has certainly applied his efforts well."

"What efforts?" Felicity asked. If she could not quite stand hearing the elder Mr. Winters praised in her hearing, she concealed it well, especially in the presence of this dead grandee's lady wife. However, she was fairly certain she kept the irritation out of her voice. The irritation at the notion that the late Mr. Winters might have done something truly good in his life.

"He has lobbied the Parliament to authorize the creation of a turnpike trust for our corner of Somerset," Mrs. Winters explained. "Before that, few people reached us, but the turnpike road has certainly made a difference. Now widow Kerr can sell Dutch cheeses and fine ribbons in her shop, and have them delivered regularly, too".

Felicity nodded, and it occurred to her that that was probably the way the elder Mr. Winters has remained in the memory of the local people—a stern but benevolent patriarch, a guardian of sorts. And, she supposed, they were not far from the truth... In a manner of speaking. Stern he certainly was, and benevolent to those he deemed to be either unthreatening outsiders far below him or the family members close to him. It was those in between, the cocksure, mercurial people too high in rank to be ignored, but too low to be useful, that felt his cold wrath upon them.

Chapter 3

'I see you are a devotee of the old style of hunting, Mr. Winters', Sir Jonathan Cadogan said as Edmund finally gained upon him. 'It's a fine thing to see in a young man'.

'That was the way my father had always hunted', Edmund replied. 'He was a hardy man, in his way. Did not believe in standing still and waiting for the game to be driven into his line of fire'.

'In that respect, your father had certainly been right. There is nothing quite like rambling over the woodland for hours on end, a good rifle in hand, looking for a hare or a rabbit or a pheasant to take down and bring home for your family. No battue can compare'.

Edmund smiled a little at Sir Jonathan's language—this lean man of middle-years had certainly been wealthy enough, if not quite as wealthy as some of his social inferiors, to send the game he shot not to the tables of his hungry family, but down to the Smithfield Market in London. The gist of his words was understandable enough, though—there was nothing quite like the satisfaction of work well done.

'Was it your father who taught you the craft of running an estate?' Sir Jonathan asked.

'In a way, yes. But, truth be told, we have both been taught by an able steward, in a way. My father wasn't born to the land. Even I was not'.

A person more skilled in social graces might have scoffed at Edmund's self-defeating frankness. Perhaps, they would have even been right. After all, reminding the man one would have liked to see as a father-in-law of such facts was probably not the wisest strategy. But Edmund had little inclination and lesser ability to say things that were not the starkest truth. His views on the matter were simple—concealing some things under a veneer of polite discourse, as he had no choice but to do with Miss Deacon, was one thing; pretending to be something he was not was another matter entirely.

'The old steward must have taught you well', Sir Jonathan admitted grudgingly. 'Your tenants certainly look well-fed'.

'It's the potatoes, Sir Jonathan. It took me years to persuade them to grow the crop—they suspected it might poison their pigs—but my example seems to have convinced them'.

For a while, no words came. Only the heavy breath of the hunters in the gray mist of the morning, the flapping of bird wings somewhere in the forest darkness, and the soft, practiced footsteps.

"I know you rather enjoy my daughter's company," Sir Jonathan said suddenly.

It was only due to the years-long training of mastering his heart and impulses that Edmund managed not to react visibly. He did, however, grasp his rifle a little more tightly. Here it came. He did not think the notion would come up so soon. He supposed, though, that men of Sir Jonathan's standing could afford to go to the heart of the matter without dancing around it.

"I do indeed", said Edmund cautiously.

"I would have asked you about your intentions, and about whether they were truly honorable. However, I know you, Edmund Winters. Whatever else one may say about you, you do not have a dishonorable bone in your body." Sir Jonathan grinned slightly. "Your intentions are quite obvious."

"Sir Jonathan, I swear I mean no harm to Miss Priscilla." He did not feel he was quite at the point yet of saying he meant to be a good husband to her. It was only belatedly that Sir Jonathan's earlier words struck him.

"Whatever they say about me?"

"You are a man of peculiar habits, they say. You care not for polite society; you care not for many things that constitute the chief delights that many people enjoy. They even say that it was your stepmother who finally had to strong-arm you into expanding the visiting rooms of Morwood Hall."

Edmund didn't reply to this. He merely stared into the distance, as though he noticed a hare there. In reality, of course, the forest continued to be silent and silver-green. It was only that what Sir Jonathan said was true. Indeed, the refurbishment of Morwood Hall had been a subject of many of Edmund's unpleasant conversations with his stepmother. She even had a thought of opening their bedrooms to visitors for the circuit the guests usually made during gatherings. He put his foot down on that matter; she did, however, get her way in quite every other thing.

"I do not quite care to be à la mode, that is true".

"This is quite an understatement, Mr. Winters. You ramble on foot so much that one might take you for a common peddler, if not a vagabond."

The subject matter struck Edmund as darkly absurd. He thought the conversation was going to be about the matter of his courting Miss Priscilla, about how his suitability as her suitor was going to rest upon the nobility of his blood (nonexistent), the nobility of his character (hopefully present), and the nobility of his intentions (fine enough). However, it seemed that Sir Jonathan had his own set of criteria—and one that Edmund did not account for.

"I do enjoy a walk in the countryside." He shrugged. "To be honest, I do not see it to be quite so very subversive as that."

"Oh, but some people may see such habit in a country squire to be subversive indeed. I am sure you have heard about Mr. Pitt's suspicions of French sympathizers our country might be harboring within".

"Our country is at peace, Sir Jonathan. They shook hands at Amiens".

"For now. God knows, the Frenchmen, they are godless bastards. Cannot trust people who would execute their own king. If there is peace, it is not for long. And even if you are right and I am wrong, I doubt this is going to make Mr. Pitt relax his policies. The days are past when long-haired youths could stride around Covent Garden and get into dangerous talks about liberty."

"Sir Jonathan, I have known some men of whom you speak while at Oxford. The only dangerous liberty they talked about was the liberty of human spirit, especially in the matters of love."

Sir Jonathan waved his free hand to indicate his general contempt for the young men in question.

"Liberty in the matters of love! What rot. Had I perfect liberty in the matters of love, my perfectly fine marriage with Priscilla's mother might have never been concluded. I imagine your father has passed good common sense to you just as mine had passed it to me, thank God".

For a while, Edmund did not reply. He thought of the day years ago, when he stood in his father's study like a schoolboy about to be punished (although, why the how? He had, indeed, been nothing but a schoolboy). He recalled his clenched fists, his sullen silence. He recalled his father's words, cold as ice and merciless as whips. But then, he hastened to remind himself, his father had not been wrong. It was not his fault he decided to give him the medicine as an original bitter drought instead of trying to sweeten it with honeyed words.

'Speaking of liberty in the matters of love', Sir Jonathan Cadogan turned to him, 'I have heard queer tidings from Morwood Hall. It is being said that a rather pretty young woman has been seen flitting around your estate. A pretty young woman of an unsteady profession, too'.

'Miss Deacon is a poetess, not a Cyprian', Edmund found himself defending her. On the other hand, what scoundrel would not have defended a young woman from such insinuations, even if whatever had existed between him and this young woman were dying embers?

'The line is very thin, sometimes. What is she to you, Winters?'

'My mother's guest. Whatever affinity had existed between us, it is long since in the past'.

'Ah, so there had been affinity between you? Let me guess, you were one of her early admirers at Oxford? The Merry One's verses about harem girls languishing with love?'

Edmund shook his head.

The meaning of the opaque pen name from her anonymous years struck him suddenly in its simplicity. The Merry One. Felicity meaning intense joy.

Clever and careless, as were most things she did.

'We used to be good friends', he said, hoping to confine the disturbance in his moods that she elicited to these six words. They used to be good friends, in the days of childhood when nothing mattered, and later in the days of early youth when everything seemed possible.

But now, they were a man and a woman grown, respectively.

Still, somehow telling Sir Jonathan that he did not desire her presence in Morwood Hall, that his stepmother had invited her without warning, seemed a peculiar betrayal. Although, why should it be? It was the perfect truth.

Felicity entered the village shop. She looked around her, amazed. There was a lot of fine haberdashery on display, and a few choice foodstuffs—tea and sugar, snuff and mustard. Fortnum and Mason it was not, for certain, but Felicity could remember the time where the village still slept in its landlocked isolation, and the only way one could get anything that was not produced locally was to go to one of the fairs, or to wait patiently for the visit of a packman with his packhorse. Felicity could still recall the day she and Edmund slipped out of the house at night—she dressed in one of his garments, her hair bound high—and departed to see the local fair. It was a merry day indeed, for they had seen what seemed to them back then to be an emporium of exotic articles.

Some of the things were almost dull, that was true. For example, the Yorkshire cloth sold in a tent with the rather plain name of The Duddery. The fares of saddlers and harness-makers did not interest the little Felicity, either. But she could not quite force herself to leave the stalls of the silk mercers and linen drapers, or the sellers of musical instruments. There was even a trader with a prodigious choice of china on display.

Of course, the pair had been discovered in the end, and soundly punished; however, the pain failed in instilling in Felicity any kind of regret for the pleasure.

"Are you looking for something?" the plump woman behind the counter asked. That must have been the widow Kerr Mrs. Winters told Felicity about.

"Yes." Felicity nodded. "I am looking for a good journal. One with paper of good quality, and, if possible, a sturdy cover".

"A journal?" the widow asked, echoing Mrs. Winters unwittingly.

"I need one to write my observations down," Felicity explained. "Things I see in the locale, and other findings of this nature".

The widow's expression furrowed in suspicion.

"What on earth are you doing such things for?"

Felicity realized that she had committed a mistake. Yes, the treaty might have been signed in Amiens, but the marrow-deep fear of French skulduggery was not to be cleared by a few signatures on a piece of paper. It was an old thing; older than the last war. Older even than the distrust toward the revolution that preceded it. She could imagine how it looked from the widow's perspective—a strange woman, finely dressed, walks into a village shop and asks to be provided with the means of observation and record! No wonder the older woman was suspicious.

"It is not what you think it is", Felicity explained. "I am not a spy. I am a poet. I hadn't left London for a long, long time, and I need to reacquaint myself with the countryside. I think writing my observations down might help me."

"From London? I don't think I've heard of any visitor from London. Or at least, none that have recently stayed at Crown and Anchor. Where are you lodging, miss?"

"I am Mrs. Williams' guest. I know you must have noticed the way I was looking at your merchandise, but it had nothing to do with any covert deals. I was merely surprised. So many things have changed since I was a girl. Why, it was only ten years ago that I remember—"

"You have lived here before, then? Are you a friend of the Cadogans?'

"God, no!' Felicity supposed someone deeming her to be from the circle of the local grandee should have flattered her. However, while the notion of Edmund Winters courting Miss Cadogan did nothing to influence her judgement, the little she knew about the father and daughter did not endear them to her. "I am, or, rather, I was Mr. Philip Deacon's daughter. He used to rent a good country house not far from Morwood Hall".

At this, widow Kerr's brow cleared.

"Felicity!" she exclaimed. "I didn't not recognize you at first! You have changed so much. You're quite a fine lady now, aren't you? I remember you had been a regular hoyden! Please, forgive me for being careful. It's only that I don't want Mr. Pitt's agents swarming all about the place. You know how it is, or, at least, how it was during the war'.

"Oh, I know it very well indeed." Felicity nodded. She recalled all the times attending dinners with the men—for they were mostly men—of the literary scene in London, the terror that hung like a cloud above the common table. Mr. Pitt's government was careful indeed about what was said, printed, written, or heard in those days.

The two women talked for a while, reminiscing about the village as it was. The widow had willingly supplied her with a tome's worth of information. Who had been wedded, who had been buried. She told her about her daughter Jane's marriage, and of the rejoicing that was when her husband returned from the French war unhurt.

"I know it usually seems to most folks that the grass was greener when they were young", Mrs. Kerr sighed. "But, truth be told, now is a sweeter life. The turnpike road, it brought us many fine things, and money besides. As for the squire in Morwood Hall—I don't want to say anything bad about the old Mr. Winters, he was not a cruel man, but…"

"But?" Felicity prodded, always a little bit gleeful to hear anyone's dissatisfaction with the late squire.

"But", the widow continued, "it's hard for me to imagine him being half as gentle as his son now is. Take, for example, the price of wheat. It was sky high while the war was on, and fell like a stone from the clouds now that there is peace. Not that I'm carping about the peace, of course, I'm not daft, but it did hit many folks in the pocket. Well, the new Mr. Winters, the young Mr. Winters, he made it so our rent was changed to be lower if the price of wheat was lower. I've heard, or at least Lily who now is the maid at Morwood Hall heard, that many of his neighbors thought him soft in the head for that, but he has always been like his father—if he took a decision, he'd stick to it'.

Felicity made herself smile, even though the joy of seeing the old acquaintance again had dimmed in her. It was silly and irrational, she knew, and unworthy of a reasonable woman to be upset so when hearing good deeds to be justly praised. However, there was something grating in the notion of the Winters, the father and the son, going forth on their merry way as benevolent masters, while she had been swept out with the dirt.

She did not know what was it that the late Mr. Winters told his son to convince the latter to bury their friendship. It might have been some hefty lie. It might have been something as simple as the press of parental authority. She knew, however, that when the decision came, it was final. The widow was right. Edward Winters was a stubborn man, but when he took a decision, he stuck to it.

Chapter 4

Edmund Winters was not sleeping. No, he was not bringing a convivial dinner party to a close, nor was he indulging in a port-fueled reverie—he was, indeed, engaged in an activity that most of his peers in the *ton* would have found incredibly boring. He was working on the estate's ledgers. Yes, he knew that they technically had a steward, but this man was old even when Edmund had seen the walls of Morwood Hall for the first time, and these days he was positively ancient, his eyesight failing. It was a good time to give the old man a pension, but finding a good replacement, and especially training that replacement afterward, would take time. And even then, frankly, Edward would probably spend some hours every week going over the estate accounts, for even in the case the new steward was an honest man, he would still be prone to errors, being, after all, a mortal, flesh and blood.

Of course, it would all be easier when Morwood Hall had a mistress. A mistress who was more concerned with actually running it than with trying to recreate the delights of the *ton* in the countryside as Abigail Winters was doing.

There were plenty of problems to occupy him on paper. The end of the war with the Revolutionary France was a blessing for many households, but a curse when it came to the farmers' livelihoods, and he had to spend plenty of time seeking ingenious ways to keep both the estate itself and the tenant homes within its bounds robust.

Edmund would not have noticed a strange vision, had he not raised his head to the windows. As it was, his caught a glimpse of the movement in the corner of his eye. In a dash, he was at the windows, looking out into the dark gardens.

His first thought was about an intruder. However, as he looked closer, he realized that what he first took for a nondescript robe was, in fact, the pale gown of the lady. Well, perhaps his stepmother was right about him being an utter ninnyhammer when it came to the accouterments of women.

Another look confirmed what he supposed—a vision of unruly black curls underneath the modish hat.

Felicity.

What on earth was she doing, going about at this hour? Yes, Morwood Hall was not exactly a den of thieves, nor a Gothic edifice from one of the popular novels. However, he would have thought that the woman who lived without her father's protection, especially in London of all places, would know well enough not to go about at this hour.

Perhaps, it occurred to him, this was precisely the reason for it. She had been confined to the seething, dangerous capital for such a long time that being transported to this green place had gone to her head like a glass of champagne.

Still, that was…simply not done. It was not done. But then, Felicity had never been exactly sensible. That is, he corrected himself, Miss Deacon was not exactly sensible. They were not children anymore. They could not simply call each other by their Christian names. They were strangers to each other, and that was how they should behave—polite strangers. Nonetheless, he felt a pinprick of guilt.

Not children anymore. One could say, they were past such easy familiarity, even back when they came apart in the first place, and simply did not realize it. She was Miss Deacon to him now, just as he was Mr. Winters to her. There was nothing to do about it.

Edmund remembered the day when his father called him into the study and gave him the blunt ultimatum. He had to drop his unseemly friendship with the Deacon girl, his father said. Naturally, Edmund bristled at such a notion back then. He used to be a regular, spirited young man, and, like all the members of the species, full of resolve to act against the tyranny of the elders, however well-meant. There were already talk, his father told him. A maid, for example, had recently overheard Mary Deacon boasting to her husband that their pretty daughter Felicity was soon going to snare the heir to Morwood and raise their family still further. Edmund only shrugged, hearing this piece of intelligence. He knew that Mary Deacon was an ambitious woman, that he had never denied; however, he was fairly certain Felicity was not a part of this. These were merely the words of the woman made giddy by the recent elevation to the mistress of a fine country house.

Even if it was so, his father told him, the sheer notion was despicable. He, Edmund, had to realize that the daughter of a minor banker—not even the master of Coutts, but of a minor establishment that was probably fated to collapse within a year or two—was not a fit playmate, much less a sweetheart, for the son of Winterses.

In response, Edward reminded his father that it was not so long ago that they were themselves nothing more than masters of the minor mercantile establishment. Wasn't it rather hypercritical of him to look down on Philip Deacon for his own position in the world?

Indeed, they were, his father had noted. Which was why they never, under any circumstances, should look backward, or allow themselves to be brought low again. The Duke of Devonshire could afford to entertain mere playwrights like Sheridan; but the Winterses were so far below such lofty heights of the *ton* that they might as well have been beggars at the gates. They had to be careful in the company they kept.

Did he, Edmund, not know how high his father had to climb, what precipices to brave, to be where he was now? Did he, Edmund, want their family to slide back into the penniless obscurity one day? For that was indeed what was going to happen if he avoided his responsibilities—social responsibilities as well as financial ones. If he so hungered for the company of people his age, why wouldn't he look to Sir Jonathan Cadogan's son? He was going to come home on an Oxford vacation soon enough, after all.

Edmund did not reply to that. He was shrewd enough to understand that his father had little hope of him ever actually befriending the older man. Why on earth, after all, would a gentleman about town pay any attention to a country bumpkin whose age would probably make him seem a mere pup? N–o—when father said that Edmund needed to pay more attention to Sir Jonathan' son, he actually meant Sir Jonathan's daughter. Back then, Edmund felt no inclination to do so. In those days, Priscilla Cadogan seemed to him haughty beyond belief. In the arrogance of youth, he did not understand the manner of those born to the privilege. The Cadogans were not peerage, that was true, but their title was old and proud enough to make the Winters surname seem like a pumpkin before a cedar tree.

"You are my only son," his father had said. "You are my greatest hope for the future. Are you going to make me proud, or are you going to turn my hopes to dust?" Of course, Edmund replied that he was going to make him proud. His nails left bloody half moons upon his palms, but did as he was told.

Edmund gazed upon the white-gowned figure in the gardens below. Although he was high above her, it seemed to him for a second she was twirling in a world of her own, and he imprisoned behind the glass.

Then he had closed the ledgers, and run downstairs.

Edmund entered the garden, and it felt as though he delved into a vat of warm milk. The night was drunk on summer; the air was warm, and filled to the brim with flowers.

And the garden was seemingly empty.

Cursing under his breath, he ran to and fro, searching for his errant guest. He wondered if Miss Deacon was prone to sleepwalking. He thought of the Lady Macbeth he saw at a theater in Bath some years ag–o—the vacant stare, the candle in hand. But the neatness of Miss Deacon's attire, at least as far as he could glimpse from the window, belied the suggestion.

He finally found her by the folly. This edifice was raised by the master of the estate long dead and gone, his bones white in the family crypt back in the days of the first George, the columns of the folly white in the night, and Felicity Deacon white in the night next to them.

Edmund called out her name, and she turned sharply, the full moon reflecting in her black pupils.

"What is the meaning of this?" he asked, marching up to her.

"I was merely taking a stroll", Miss Deacon replied.

"At night? It is hardly safe".

She shrugged.

"I do not think there are many dangers that can assail me on the grounds of Morwood Hall. Unless, of course, you know otherwise."

"There are poachers prowling the woods".

"I supposed so, too, which is why I did not go into the woods. I'm not completely soft in the head. I went to the gardens. Now, if I went out of bounds as a guest, if my walks are to be confined to the space around the cottage, I would appreciate it if you tell me so; but I would be grateful if you indeed say it openly."

"Of course, you have the run of the gardens," he said. "We are not your wardens. But we are your hosts. You might catch cold. You are dressed very lightly, after all".

"I doubt anyone can catch a cold on such a fine summer evening".

"Summer warmth could be deceptive. It evaporates as soon as the sun sets. No memory of it remains. Believe me, I know".

"You are a very caring host." Miss Deacon smiled. "No one would have thought that, not so long ago, you were bristling at my presence in Morwood Hall".

"It is not that I did not want you here", Edmund started, "it was only that I was surprised by your arrival".

He realized that he was indeed telling her a complete truth, not a polite fiction. Or at least, something that had transmuted into truth by now, even if it had not been entirely so back then. Yes, he knew that between him as he was now and the him that could take Priscilla Cadogan down the aisle there lay a number of obstacles, but he knew now that Felicity Deacon was not one of them, and did not deserve his irritation, much less his ire. The greatest obstacle, if anything, was his own nature. He wondered if his stepmother had been right in chastising him for shunning the *ton*, and if he might do well to listen to her suggestions, if he was going to win the Cadogans over.

That being said, he knew he was not going to turn his bedroom over to the amusement of guests. Of that, he was certain.

"What on earth propelled you to go out of doors at such an hour, anyway?" Edmund asked meanwhile.

"It is hard to say", Felicity replied. "But... Have you ever felt that on certain nights, the blooms are just burning with scent, and the world seems to be more alive than ever? It seems a travesty to sleep on such a night. An insult to God's creation".

There was something giddy in her now; something peculiarly re-laxed at the same time. Perhaps, it was the darkness; perhaps, it was the moonlight, but she looked several years younger than she was in truth, and more at ease with the world than she had been during any of their previous conversations since her arrival.

Edmund himself had always been a creature of daylight, red-eyed vigils over ledgers notwithstanding. His was the world of morning hunts, afternoon rambles, early breakfasts. As far as he was concerned, nights were for sleeping. Now, had he thought differently, he was fairly certain that few people would have reproached him, him being a young man with a considerable fortune. He knew several gentleman answering the same description who made it their business to turn night into day. Miss Deacon, however, being a woman, would not have faced quite the same reaction. Indeed, if someone was told that this woman rather preferred night to day, and the world of darkness to the world of light, they would usually make suppositions about her character that were none too flattering.

He did not want anyone to suppose Felicity Deacon to be anything but virtuous.

It was not, however, in his power to correct her habits. The only thing he could do now was to keep her safe and warm.

"I propose a compromise", Edward said. "Perhaps, I could accompany you back to the Lavender Cottage. That way, you would be able to see and enjoy the landscape, while I will be sure that I have conveyed you to safety. I promise to walk very slowly", he added as he saw her part her lips a little to say something in response.

For a second, Felicity Deacon was silent. Her face was a Greek mask, almost white in the light of the moon. It looked very dramatic next to her dark hair, and looked as though she was transformed into some grandiose figure of myth.

Then she looked up at him, the corners of her mouth lifting a little, and the illusion was shattered. She was her living, impish self again.

"Well, you are my host, and the stepson of my patroness. It would be ill of me, not to mention ungrateful, to spurn your care".

They walked in silence for a while. Of course, silence was not quite the right term. The night was alive with the chirping of insects. Somewhere, in the distant wood, an owl hooted.

Miss Deacon was the first one to break the silence.

'Is your library still as wonderful as it used to be?' she asked, turning her head to him. The moonlight was tinting her skin faint blue, turning her into a pearl glowing under the sea.

'I hope so'.

'You hope so, Mr. Winters?' Miss Deacon teased. 'Does it mean you have not paid it a visit for some time?'

'For a rather long time, I am afraid. My duties leave me little time for Homer'.

In truth, he had not been quite as intoxicated as she by the writings of the bard from Chios even when he had been a youth with romantic notions. He did read both epics, however, because Felicity Deacon devoured them, and he never wanted to be left behind and alone without Felicity Deacon by his side.

They really used to be bosom-friends.

'I thought your father had decreased his interests in trade?'

'He did.' Edmund nodded. 'But land requires as much work, and as much understanding of commerce, if not more...' He paused. 'Forgive me. I must be boring you'.

'Not at all. I have always been interested in how things work, beneath the shining surface of the world'.

Edmund knew she was probably speaking so out of courtesy, nothing else. For what lady in the world, fresh from the capital, would be genuinely engrossed in the business-minded ramblings of an uncouth squire?

'Is there anything new to hear in London?' he inquired quickly, cutting himself off the temptation to take her up on her invitation and spend the walk to the Lavender Cottage rambling about potato harvests.

'Oh, every day'.

'But there must be some chief subject of conversation, surely?'

'Apart from His Majesty's health... They are saying the peace treaty is paper thin, and won't last long'.

Felicity Deacon's tone as she said these words wasn't grave, nor was it nonchalant. There was a curious dull quality to it, as though she were a woman so used to the wickedness of the world it had numbed her to misfortunes.

Perhaps she is, his inner voice whispered. *How do you know what happened to her since you said goodbye to her last in the gardens of Morwood Hall?*

'Is it certain?'

'Nothing is certain in that place.' She shrugged. 'Everything is written in water, and the chess pieces are made of butter. But I think it more likely than not. Besides, it's not as though the French themselves are meek lambs. I have heard some people speak, people who have gone to France and returned. There are talks of fresh conquests there, too'.

'That is a tragedy in the making, if so. The people have already been bled dry. What is Mr. Pitt going to do, build ships from their bones?'

'I rather think he is going to be building ships out of something else. But you know the species of the local trees better than I do. Of course, you don't have to listen to me', Miss Deacon added before he had a chance to reply. 'I am merely a scribbler'.

'Miss Deacon...' Edmund started.

'Forgive me'. She lowered her eyelashes, and it seemed more exhaustion than coquetry. 'I do not know what I am saying. It's like some *Abgrund*'.

'Some what?'

'*Abgrund*. It's German for...like a chasm'.

'A fissure in the ground?'

'More like an abyss. Their poets are somewhat obsessed with the word. It means...something dark, wild, primordial. Something you would encounter in the deep recesses of Alps. Hardly in Somerset'. Miss Deacon smiled then, and there was something polished and ready about her smile, as though she extracted it from some drawer just for an occasion of this sort. 'And, in any case, I merely meant the chasm

I sometimes feel between what I want to say and the words that come out of my mouth'.

'You are a poet', Edmund commented with some incredulity, and found himself teasing her a little. 'If you cannot shape your words properly, where is the hope for the rest of us?'

'Oh, I can! On paper. Thank God the days of Homer and Sappho are past. I would not have lasted one evening improvising my poems out of this air for a listening audience. I need time to prepare. To craft everything well'.

Abgrund. Yes, that was the right word for the space between them, a jagged abruptness in every vowel, even before one got to the meaning.

He had to bridge it somehow, Edmund realized. Otherwise the coming months they had to spend in such close proximity were going to become unbearable.

The walls of the Lavender Cottage rose ahead of him, solid in the night, and final as though they themselves have been a sort of an abyss.

He didn't have much time left to issue his...not quite an apolog–y—an apology required a misdeed, he told himsel–f—but an explanation.

'I remember the last time I saw you in these gardens', Edmund began.

'I have been almost a child then'. Felicity Deacon looked away.

'So have I. Miss Deacon, I need you to know the reasons for my...behavior on that day'.

'The day when you saw fit to tell me we could see each other no longer?'

'Yes. Exactly'.

'You gave me your reasons on that very day, Mr. Winters. You thought me an unseemly companion, and...'

'I am sure I did not put it like that'.

'Your father did, then, and you said you did not want to go against his will'.

'I want you to know, it was not out of any dislike for you, Miss Deacon. Not on my father's part, and certainly not on my own. He had been worried that something...untoward might happen'.

'Something that might jeopardize your standing in society?'

'He had heard your mother claim that she...had designs on me as her possible son-in-law. I know you are not her, have never been her, but to him, it was the last straw that broke the camel's back'.

'Yes', Miss Deacon said quietly. 'That does sound like Mother'.

Edmund expected a fiery argument, something in defense of Mary Deaco–n—who had, after all, taken evident good care of her daughter after her husband's death. But no argument ensued. The night was silent.

He wondered if, perhaps, that care had not been as good as it might seem; if Mrs. Deacon had even mistreated her daughter in some way.

The thought of it made him suddenly want to clasp Felicity Deacon's hand, or even to press her against him protectively, to promise that, while Morwood Hall was no idyll, no one was going to harm her while she was here.

However, the notion was patently absurd, not to mention improper.

'This seems to be the Lavender Cottage', Edmund said, his words sounding even to himself a mere string of cowardliness. 'I hope you have a good night's sleep...Miss Deacon'.

'I hope you do, too, Mr. Winters.' The ironic quirk to a corner of her mouth was hard to miss. 'It seems like you need it. Your eyes are rimmed with red'.

'Perhaps. I don't look in the mirror very often'.

'Then you should. Or, perhaps, you could simply take the opinion of others on the matter into account'.

'Believe me, Miss Deacon, taking the opinion of others into account is one of my chief habits'.

'I know'. She turned the key in the lock. 'Believe me, Mr. Winters, I know'.

Then she stepped into the cottage, and slowly disappeared in the unlit darkness of the rooms beyond.

Chapter 5

'You look invigorated today', Abigail Winters remarked over breakfast. 'Had I not known you as well as I do, I might have supposed you spent the night either in solid rest or in a bout of bracing revelry. But, of course, you are too industrious by half for the former, and too proper for the latter'.

'It is merely the promise of the fine day, Mother. Although, I do have some plans that I am rather looking forward to'.

'I am intrigued'.

'I think to have elms planted in Morwood'.

'How very exciting', Mrs. Winters responded, deadpan. 'May I ask why?'

'They are much preferred by the navy when it comes to ship-building. Besides, compared to oaks, they do not take much time to grow. I have it on good account that the kind of wood suitable for ships might be in demand a few years hence'.

'On whose good account?'

Edmund hesitated. He did not want to divulge the story of his strange nighttime walk with Miss Deacon. After all, that would have meant betraying why he was down in the gardens at night in the first place, and thus the secret of Felicity Deacon's peculiar walks. On the other hand, complete secrecy did not agree with him.

'Miss Deacon shared some news from the capital with me. There are talks of the fragility of the peace'.

'God help us'.

'I hope He will. But it does not mean we should not take some measures ourselves'.

'Are you sure Miss Deacon is such a good source? I am not saying she might be not speaking the truth as far as she is concerned, but she is not the kind of woman members of Parliament confide in'.

'One does not need to sit in the House of Commons to feel the way the wind is blowing, Mother', Edmund said with sharpness that surprised even himself. 'Miss Deacon has a good ear. I trust her'.

'Goodness. And to think that less than two weeks ago you were willing to twist my arm only to cut her stay in Lavender Cottage short'.

'It was a rash response, and I regret it'.

'That is fine of you. Although, I have to say, I do wish you spent less time thinking about elm-planting and the like. It is all fine and good for a gentleman to take interest in his estate, but he cannot cut himself off from the society of his peers completely'.

'If this is a hint that I ought to permit you to enlarge our rooms for the reception of guests, you already know my answer to this'.

The newfangled design—a circle of three well-decorated rooms on top of a grand staircase—had been Mrs. Winters' idea. It was finished within the last few years of her husband's life, and, although he rather encouraged it, as he had encouraged all endeavors that could endear the Winterses to the *ton*, his son was cut from a different cloth. While he accepted the addition to the old structure of Morwood Hall, Edmund had put his foot down when it came to the notion of adding two or three more rooms to the circuit.

'It is still unchanged, then? It is quite a shame. We cannot hide in the wilderness as though we were the boorish squires of the past century, with William and Mary still on the throne. I don't want us to become the sort of landowners comedians parody on London stage'.

'I do not want us to become a place of noisy gatherings, either'.

'I do wonder what Priscilla Cadogan would say of your stance on the matter, Edmund. I imagine, being Sir Jonathan's daughter, she is rather used to noisy gatherings in her honor'.

His stepmother was probably right on this count, Edmund realized. His father had been invited to more dinners at Sir Jonathan's fine estate than he himself had been, but even so, it was plain that the Cadogans' house was quite a place of gaiety.

'To think of it', Mrs. Winters pressed, 'what reason, exactly, does Sir Jonathan have to betroth his daughter to you? Or the daughter in question to give her consent to the suit, for that matter? I imagine she would be asked, at the very least'.

'I can offer her great comfort, and a good care'.

'She has great comfort in her father's house, too. It is not as though he were one of those penniless knights who are always in debt. If anything, it is others who are in debt to him. Not us, of course', she added quickly, seeing Edmund's alarmed expression, 'but plenty of people, and not only in Somerset. He can find a suitor for his daughter from farther afield. Next summer, he is going to give her a proper London Season, and it is likely to be a success'.

'I cannot comprehend why are you laying out my inadequacies on the breakfast table', Edmund said stiffly.

'I am merely saying that, if your mind it truly set on this match, you could at least make an effort to impress her. If we were, for instance, to organize a ball..."

Ah. Now his stepmother's scheme was clear as day. She did not suddenly change her mind about the Cadogan match, she was merely using it as a lever to induce her stepson to give some magnificent entertainment. The lengths to which Mrs. Winters could go to alleviate what she called the country boredom were truly astonishing.

Fortunately for her scheme, Edmund was in a surprisingly good this morning, his blood running quicker than usual. Partly it had to do with the elm-related plans, partly with yesterday's walk with Miss Deacon. While he did not believe the talent for organizing country balls was all that important in a suitor compared to his sobriety, prosperity, and moral soundness, he was willing to indulge his stepmother's love for amusements.

'Well and good." Edmund nodded, and enjoyed the flicker of surprise on Mrs. Winters' face. 'We might do just that'.

'Here I was prepared for a long battle!' Mrs. Winters brightened. 'Oh, but there is much to do. I hope you will talk to Miss Deacon on the subject'.

'To invite her, you mean?'

'Do you think we should?'

'I think it would be rather thoughtless of us to exclude our guest. Do you not think so, Mother?'

'I suppose so. But I rather meant, you could ask her advice. I am sure she has seen how the best people in London organize such evenings. Perhaps, she could finally prevail upon you...'

'Even if she does, I highly doubt we could add two rooms to the house in time for the ball, unless you mean to give it next summer',

Edmund said caustically. 'But, since that is your wish, I am going to talk to her on the subject'.

The first feeling that flooded Felicity when she opened her eyes in the morning and recalled the events of the night before was shame.

What on earth was she thinking indeed, striding about at night alone like a Cyprian soliciting patrons in pleasure gardens? Perhaps, it was the fault of the heady summer night, with its smell of cow parsley and honeysuckle in the air. Perhaps, though, it was merely the intoxication of nostalgia. Morwood Hall used to be her childhood playground, after all, and the repository of her youthful dreams.

She blushed furiously as she washed her face. She could well imagine what Edmund Winters was thinking about her now, for all his stiff outward courtesy.

Perhaps, Felicity thought, it would be better to spend the day indoors, just to make sure she did not accidentally run into the master of Morwood Hall and thus did not combust into a ball of roaring flame with embarrassment.

Felicity sat at the desk and opened the journal she had bought in Mrs. Kerr's shop. She paused before putting pen to paper. Even now, when her only duty was to pour forth natural reflections of what she had seen, she could not get rid of the habit to churn the thoughts in her head first until they were spic and span and gleaming with polish.

No one is going to see this, Felicity reminded herself. *This is for your eyes only, to use as fuel for your writings later on.*

Her eyes strayed to the letter sitting on the edge of her desk. She did not read it fully yet—she did not need to. She could guess the later contents by the first paragraph.

Mr. Flyte was unhappy. And when her agent was not happy, it did not take a genius to guess that she had a chance of being made very unhappy indeed. After all, he was the proprietor of the small but influential *Fine-Letters Gazette* That, indeed, was how he had first made her acquaintance.

Well, not quite. Felicity was not stupid enough that, when he first looked at her in Drury Lane Theater, Mr. Flyte was concerned with discerning her literary talent.

Despite the warmth of the summer day, a thin, glacial shiver ran down Felicity's spine.

She needed to crawl out of the chasm, the *Abgrund*, where she had driven herself. She needed to write again, and soon.

There was plenty of foxglove... Felicity wrote down clumsily. *Foxglove hanging heavy and purple, its petals like a Roman imperial mantle. Around the hawthorns, the air was cream-sweet...*

Heavens above, this—writing down minute observations that were going to become fuel for her future verses—was harder than she had anticipated. Was it that she had gotten so used to the bright spectacles of magnificence—masquerades at the Pantheon, shows at Astley's Amphitheatre, the dappled stallions of grandees on Rotten Row—that smaller, paler things now escaped her attention?

That thought was interrupted by a knock upon the door. Not without some relief, Felicity rushed to open it.

Edmund Winters was standing on the doorstep, and in his hands he was holding a book.

'Mr. Winters." Felicity blinked. 'Good day to you'.

'Miss Deacon', he cleared his throat, 'I have brought you a small gift'.

'Oh, you did not have to...' But, even as she was said these words, her eyes were straying toward the cover, straining to read the title.

'I feel I very much did', Edmund Winters said, and offered her the tome.

Now, Felicity could see the title very well indee–d—and the author's name, too.

Her breath caught.

'Milton, *Paradise Lost*? But—isn't it from your father's library?'

'It is indeed'.

'And yet you are offering it to me?'

'So far as I know, my father has never touched it'.

'Nonetheless, he must be turning in his grave now', Felicity noted before she could bite her tongue.

To her surprise, Edmund did not frown, and neither did he scold her in response to saying so about the memory of his sainted sire.

'I doubt he would have mourned the book all that much', he said evasively.

'Why did he buy it, then? Books are not cheap. Much of my own income comes from circulating libraries'.

It was, perhaps, vulgar to speak of such lowly matters as income, but Felicity sensed Edmund Winters would not mind. After all, given his own excited speech on the matters of the land yesterday night, he was a man who took his own bookkeeping very seriously indeed.

I have not been particularly privy to his thoughts. But he has always been...' Mr. Winters paused, clearly weighing his words, 'avid to fit himself to the tastes of those he thought his betters'.

'And to fit others to these tastes, too'.

'It is not as though he had taxed me with Virgil overmuch when I was a boy'.

'No, that was my own task', Felicity teased.

He smiled in response, taking her breath away.

For a second, it was as though the years in between them had dissolved in the ether. It was as though they had both become younger again, not twenty yet, their skins still tender-thin, their hearts fearless.

The illusion did not last long. Edmund Winters' smile dimmed as he coughed.

'I have to confess to the true reason of my visit, Miss Deacon'.

Felicity's heart fell a little. Of course there was a true reason. Of course he would not call upon her in her cottage merely for the sake of seeing her face and giving her a present. What on earth was she thinking about?

Gifts were more than gifts, after all—she had had years to learn that. Oh, she supposed there was a world somewhere where they were truly nothing but expressions of true affection, but she suspected this world was beyond the mortal touch. It certainly was beyond hers. Here, on earth, they were either expressions of favor...or requests for one.

Only, what kind of favor would the master of Morwood Hall want from her, of all people?

'I am all ears'.

'My mother has an idea to give a ball at Morwood, and I have agreed to do just that. But I wonder if...' Edmund Winters paused. Was he truly fumbling for words like schoolboy? 'If you would be so kind as to...'

'I will help you, of course', Felicity put him out of his misery, 'but what kind of help would you even need?'

'Nothing onerous, I assure you. I am merely interested to hear how such things are done in London these days. I would not want to appear uncouth in front of our neighbors'.

'In front of the Cadogans, you mean?' Felicity asked bluntly.

'They are indeed going to be invited', Edmund Winters replied stiffly.

'I have heard there is a...friendship between your families now'.

'It is not as though we have ever feuded'.

'No, I suppose not', Felicity replied as evenly as she could. She knew she was being ridiculous, but... It was not as though she disliked the notion of Edmund Winters marrying at al–l—that would have been absurd—but there was something particularly insulting about him marrying Priscilla Cadogan of all people.

Why so? her inner voice asked. *Just because you regard your childhood as some unspoiled pool of purity and tranquility, it does not mean he has to do the same. He is a man grown, and is perfectly at liberty to shed the past. Come to think of it, he has already done so.*

'I am going to help you, of course, Mr. Winters', Felicity added. 'After all, it would be boorish of me not to do so for my betters, especially since you have been so kind to me, little though I deserve it'.

She did not have to use a roaring, flaming sword to cut.

Chapter 6

'I think', Felicity proclaimed after a turn around an empty French-style saloon, 'what this room lacks is an Aeolian harp'.

Edmund Winters winced.

'I know my mother went too far in the decoration, but, please, do not mock her efforts'.

'I am doing nothing of the sort. I really think an Aeolian harp would lend refinement to these guest chambers'.

'Mother does not play a harp'.

'Oh, she does not have to! It would merely need to stand here, and proclaim to everyone that a lady of fine sensibilities lives in this house'.

'Why an Aeolian harp, of all things? Why not a regular one?'

'It is linked in every mind with the ancient poetess Sappho', Felicity explained. 'Some poets of old Rome called her the Tenth Muse'.

'In every mind, Miss Deacon?' Mr. Winters stressed the second word, raising his eyebrows. 'Or merely in the minds of men and women reared in Mayfair?'

'Well, perhaps not in every mind', Felicity conceded, 'but certainly in most. It is a little like a turban on the head of a hostess. A thing of fashion'.

'A turban, too?'

'Ever since Madame de Stael started wearing one across the Channel, many a lady of the *ton* followed her example. They wanted to hint at their...'

'Fine sensibilities?' Edmund Winters asked, his face seemingly impassive, but his eyes glimmering with good humor.

'See, you are learning already!' Felicity laughed. 'Give me but a year, and I am going to make you a veritable man-about-town'.

A pause. An unseen, silent chasm. She realized abruptly that this little joke was hopeless, because in a year's time she was going to be back in London, under Mr. Flyte's thumb, and Mr. Winters... Mr. Winters was likely going to be married, and to a lady whom, from what Felicity knew of her, would suffer no Aeolian harps in her home.

'I see it's a dangerous thing to give you the rule, then, Miss Deacon'.

'You did ask for my advice', Felicity pointed out.

'I did not say I am not going to take it. As long as you do not threaten to next dress me as a Turk or my mother as an odalisque'.

'From what little I know of Mrs. Winters, I am not so sure she is going to be that averse to the idea'.

'Oh, she won't be. Which is why I really must ask you never to bring it up in her presence'.

'I would not dare', Felicity teased him back, elated suddenly.

Perhaps, it was the sun streaming from the windows, the light touching Mr. Winters' face and softening his features. Perhaps, it was simply the joy of being...almost back where she once was. Almost as though Morwood Hall had been her home once, her lost Ithaca, and not the much more modest country house in the vicinity where her father visited and her mother schemed.

'What kinds of dances are you going to have during the ball?' Felicity asked.

'Allemande and the French cotillion, I imagine'.

'What about Moll in the Wad?'

'About what?'

'I cannot wager if it is danced in every ballroom in town yet, of course—I have not been to every ballroom in town, however much I wished to—but it has certainly been danced in a few good ones'.

'I am afraid I have not heard of it'.

'Would you like me to teach you?'

'We have no music'.

'I will mark the rhythm with my voice'.

For a second, it seemed to Felicity that Mr. Winters was going to decline. However, to her surprise, he nodded.

'I give myself into your hands, Miss Deacon'.

'That's a good start', Felicity joked. 'Now, there is nothing especially complicated. It's a quick country dance. We are to stand opposite one another, then we are to link hands, and...' Not waiting for Mr. Winters to do just that, Felicity glided across the floor, painting a star-shape with her feet. 'Then we skip around for a while, and after that...'

Edmund Winters raised his arm, as though a perfect pupil.

'I think', he said, 'before we move in to that part, we should first perfect the first movement'.

'If you insist', Felicity breathed. She liked the dance, and her legs were itching to carry it on, again and again and again.

She stepped closer to the man who had once been her closest friend, and he offered her his arm, as though they were to walk in the silent garden together once more.

Felicity linked her arm with his.

She had a strange relationship with dancing—the steps and the movement she had always enjoyed, but the touch of her flesh to her partner's often made her shiver, if not recoil, especially if the partner's grip was proprietary. She knew the reason, of course.

Mr. Winters' hold, however, was light, if firm. There was something soothing in it, like a reassurance that, if she fell—and not just in the way of literal mishaps during dancing—he would be there to catch her.

'Like this', she whispered, 'a few skips around to start with'.

'I have to confess, country dances have always made me feel perfectly foolish. I am not a man much suited to skipping around'.

'I think everyone should do some skipping around from time to time. It stretches muscles and minds'.

'You certainly have a way with words'.

'Well, that is how I earn my living, isn't it?'

She shouldn't have said it, she knew, as soon as the words were out of her mouth. Now, when it seemed for a moment she was almost his equal, sharing a dance to invisible music as though she herself had been the daughter of a local gentry, why did she have to ruin the illusion by reminding him what she was?

However, Edmund Winters didn't seem to recoil from the reminder, or even to stiffen at it. Instead, he repeated the steps Felicity had shown him, albeit in a very clumsy fashion.

'Your skipping certainly wants some practice, Mr. Winters." Felicity turned her head to look into his face, straining her neck a little. It occurred to her that she had not seen him this close ever since the days they were mock-fighting in the meadows around Morwood Hall, many years ago. Except, Edmund Winters—who had been simply Edmund in those days—had not been half as pleasant to look at back then as he was now. Or, perhaps, it was simply that Felicity's mind was on different things back then, and she did not notice how fine the firm features of his face were, or how arresting the hazel specks in his gray eyes.

'I am glad you don't think me a completely hopeless pupil'.

'I will be glad to teach you. But I have to say, I cannot promise miracles in weeks'.

'You do not believe in miracles, then?'

'Do you?'

Silence stretched between them, taut as a harp's string poised for singing.

'Sometimes, when the belief is warranted. I think it is, in this case. If all else fails', Mr. Winters added, 'you could give me the very last lesson on the day of the ball, just before we all go to see the guests'.

Felicity's heard skipped a beat.

'We?'

He blinked.

'Has mother not told you?'

'You don't mean I am invited?'

'Of course you are. I hope you didn't think me such a monster of discourtesy as to leave you out'.

"I..." What was Felicity to say? That she had already resigned to the conviction that he was going to do just that? That she knew that masked balls at the Pantheon with their paid subscriptions were one thing, and private affairs of the squires another, and a woman who could buy her way into the former was not necessarily invited to the latter? That she was, indeed, quite sure he would do his utmost to see to it that his future bride and his past sweetheart would never meet in such a setting? 'I would be honored to come'.

'Does the village happen to have a carrier?' Felicity was breathing fast, since her walk to the shop was almost a half-run. Panic was beating at her wrists.

The widow Kerr looked at her state with some surprise.

'It does. Do you need something brought from town?'

'A—some of my things, back from home'.

'What manner of things?'

'A ballgown', Felicity confessed. 'I have one or two at home. In London, I lodge with my mother, and she should have no trouble finding one to give to the carrier, and—'

'A ballgown!' the shopkeeper exclaimed. 'Why would you need one, here?'

'Mr. Winters is giving a ball, and he... He has been kind enough to invite me'.

'Mr. Winters, giving a ball! A comet must have passed through the skies, and I didn't notice. I wonder whatever induced him'.

'I did not choose anything suitable with me, when I was packing for Somerset. I knew I was not going to venture into Bath, and I... I thought that, even if my hosts are going to organize something of the kind, they would never see fit to invite me'.

'Oh, Felicity. You are thinking ill of Mr. Winters. He is all precise and proper, that's true, but he has never done an insult to anyone'.

'It would not have been an insult', Felicity said quietly. 'Only a natural order of things'.

To her surprise, the widow came out from behind the counter and grasped Felicity's hand in her plump, calloused fingers.

'Sweet girl, who has hurt you so very terribly?'

Something painful pierced Felicity's being, like a shock of wine thrown upon a wound. For a second, she was tempted to confess everything—everything that happened since she left Morwood Hall for the last time as a bawling girl; for what she thought was the last time. Everything that happened later, since her father died.

Fortunately, she came to her senses quickly. This was a small village, and such places were always hotbeds of gossip.

She put a smile on.

'Why, no one. I am merely stating a fact'.

Mrs. Kerr looked at her with some doubt, but did not press the questioning.

'Our carrier set out for London not two days past. It is going to be some time until he reaches the town, finishes his business there, comes back, sets out once more. How much time is there until the ball?'

Felicity's heart fell.

'Two weeks at most'.

'Hm. That's not long enough. Tell you what—my daughter is very quick with a needle, and I have some good cloth on sale here. How about you'll have a new gown made with my Jane?'

Felicity swallowed, imagining the cost of a completely new garment as opposed to the one of merely bringing her old one up from the city.

But the alternative was not going to Morwood Hall on the night of the ball at all. The sheer notion of leaving all these people to laugh and dance in the amber light of candles while she was watching the glimmering in the far-off windows like fireflies was unbearable.

'I would be grateful', she said. 'Though, I imagine, your daughter is very busy?'

'She is', the older woman told her frankly, 'but she'll find some time for you. Truth be told, her husband hasn't been the same since he returned from the war. Tremor in his hands. She'll be glad to have a

nice way of earning something for the family on the side. After all',
she added, 'us women, we have to be resourceful, don't we?'

Chapter 7

Mrs. Winters invited Felicity to take a dish of tea with her in Morwood Hall proper the very next afternoon.

For the first hour, time flew with steady sweetness, like a river of honey. Felicity was not sure how much Milton or Pope her hostess had read, so she made her best effort not to overwhelm her with references. She did not eliminate them entirely, however. Those literary patrons who were not interested in poetry in general usually helped its authors out of desire to feel themselves men and women of culture and importance. It would not have been wise of Felicity to accept said patronage on such terms, and then talk about nothing but fripperies.

Not that she had anything against fripperies. Indeed, she rather enjoyed them. But a conversation, much like a reading, had to be tailored to a particular audience. A wealthy bluestocking like Lady Montagu, or a highborn hostess like the Duchess of Devonshire, could afford to speak their mind nearly always, but Felicity had no such luxury.

She was just telling Abigail Winters of the old Italian tradition of an improvisatrice, a kind of female bard performing for crowds and courts alike, and how she had a mind to write a poem on the subject, when a sudden visit was announced.

'Sir Jonathan and Miss Priscilla Cadogan?' Mrs. Winters repeated, as the footman opened the door to the withdrawing room. 'Why, I wonde..."

She looked...unsettled. Nervous, but not pleasantly so. This was not the voice of a woman anxious to meet her future daughter-in-law.

'I think it would be better if I go." Felicity rose.

'That's sheer nonsense. I am not ashamed of your company. There is nothing to be ashamed of! Besides, I would dearly like to hear more about—"

The young widow never did finish the sentence, because at that moment, the pair entered the room.

Sir Jonathan did not differ much from Felicity's recollections of the man. When she had been a child in Somerset, the chief thing she seemed to have noticed about him was his astonishingly colorful waistcoats. Now, in accordance with the new fashion, the color of his garments had faded into something more somber (or, she added irreverently in her thoughts, penguin-like). The figure became more imposing, and the face more florid. However, the air of a man who felt a kind of mastery over all his surroundings had not changed.

His daughter, Miss Priscilla Cadogan, wore a lavender frock in the way of a half-dress. It was made of the finest cambric Felicity had ever seen, and the sight made her as uncomfortable in her own linen gown as if it had been made of raw wool.

Felicity did not have much time to muse on the difference in the appearances, because, quickly enough, Miss Cadogan's gaze alighted on her.

'I do not believe we have been introduced', Priscilla Cadogan told her, her smile glowing, yet distant.

'This is Miss Felicity Deacon', Mrs. Winters rushed to tell her. 'A fine poetess who does me the honor of being my guest this summer. Miss Deacon, this is Miss Priscilla Cadogan'.

As if someone blew out a candle, Miss Cadogan's smile dimmed.

'A poetess', she repeated. 'How interesting'.

'You have probably heard her name', Mrs. Winters added helpfully.

'I might have'.

'Do you dislike the genre?' Felicity asked as politely as she could. Whatever her own feelings on the subject, she had to make the best impression on her patroness...and on Mr. Winters.

Because, after all, he was the master of the estate, she reminded herself hastily. It would be unwise to carp like a fishwife in his presence. Even if she wanted to.

'Not at all." Miss Cadogan shook her head as she sat. 'I am only surprised to...see a poetess in the flesh, especially in such surprising circumstances'.

This was not the response of a literary lover awed at the notion of meeting a writer in person. Felicity had seen the real article several times—including in Mrs. Winters—and would have known it if she encountered it.

Miss Cadogan might have had nothing against putting pen to paper, or even earning one's bread with it, but she clearly didn't think such a person had to be received in a good house.

'I don't see what is so surprising about these circumstances', Edmund Winters said suddenly, softly. 'Miss Deacon is our honored guest. It would have been churlish of us never to invite her to join us here'.

'Perhaps." Sir Jonathan nodded. 'I merely wonder if she would not be bored with our company. After all, she has likely led a much more exciting life alone in London'.

Felicity's cheeks grew hot. She was not an idiot. She knew what respectable men, especially men such as Sir Jonathan, thought of the morals of single women who 'led exciting lives' in anonymous, glittering cities.

'I don't live alone', she said quickly, and hated herself for scrambling for the arguments of defense so. 'When in London, I lodge with my widowed mother'.

'Do you indeed? What does your mother think about your work?'

'She is entirely supportive of it'.

Or, at least, she became so, once she realized that Felicity's quill might become their ticket. If not to the former prosperity, then at least to some semblance of comfort.

Mary Deacon had always been a most pragmatic woman.

'I remember the frequency with which Miss Deacon's verse appeared in *Fine-Letters Gazette* from the start', Mr. Winters pointed out. 'There are few people I know who work as hard as her'.

Felicity looked at him with surprise, unable to contain herself. Was he truly defending her?

She had been certain to the bone that, for all their recent pleasantries, when push came to shove, he was going to choose his highborn potential bride over the nobody that was her.

But he wasn't choosing her, Felicity reminded herself, bringing herself back down to earth. Words were a quick and cheap coin.

'I have no doubt Miss Deacon has to work a lot to keep such a prodigious output up', Miss Cadogan replied politely, probably sensing she had gone a trifle too far.

Not that these words were devoid of barbs. Felicity knew without needing to be told that, for the likes of Cadogans, people fortunate enough to boast wealth as well as a title, someone having to work every day to keep the roof over her head was all in itself shudder-inducing.

'Are there particular poets you like?' Mrs. Winters interjected in a valiant attempt to steer the conversation back to safe waters.

'I've enjoyed Claire Miles when I was still at schoolroom." Miss Cadogan shrugged. 'I recall how surprised I was to learn that she was no older than me when she had published her first book of verse'.

Claire Miles.

The withdrawing room could have been emptied of all air for a second, and Felicity would have felt no different.

'Do you know her?' Abigail Winters turned her head to her. 'You have mentioned that the London literary scene is often as small and tight-knit as a village'.

'I have...heard of her', Felicity said carefully. Her mouth was dry.

'You have not met her?'

'Maybe once or twice. She... Her star was on the decline by the time I had reached some success'.

'I wonder if these events had something to do with each other'.

Fear, sharp as a needle. Nausea that had nothing to do with an empty stomach. Head spinning.

She could not know. Mrs. Winters could not know. She was, by her own admission, quite marooned in the quietude of the country-side—indeed, that was one of the reasons she had invited Felicity for the summer in the first place.

But what if it was not true? What if she was well-appraised of some things indeed, and her invitation was not a blithe kindness, but a subtle cruelty—an attempt to show her stepson just how right he had been to discard his unsuitable connection?

This blind terror lasted a few heartbeats, each spawning more wild theories than the last. Then, however, Felicity forced herself to breathe slowly to calm down. Abigail Winters was a woman as far removed from Machiavellian schemes as it was possible to be. Besides, what would have been the point of such a game? Would it not have been easier and more sensible to simply refrain from the invitation, allowing Felicity and Mr. Winters to orbit their own planets in peace? They would not have met again in that case.

'Miss Deacon, are you quite all right?' Edmund Winters asked her, watching her with attention and—almost a palpable worry.

'Of course', Felicity managed to say. 'I have never been better'.

'Are you sure? You are rather pale'.

'I have never thought artistic rivalry could be such a mighty force', Priscilla Cadogan chimed in. 'If the mention of Miss Miles distresses Miss Deacon so, I promise to refrain from talking about other poets in the future'.

This young woman was just incapable of not delivering a stab when someone's flank was open, it seemed.

'Your concern touches my heart', Felicity said dryly, looking at her. 'I think, it might be better if I leave your company for a while', she told Mrs. Winters.

'That would be a shame. Are you sure you are not unwell?'

'Perhaps, a touch. I might need some fresh air'.

As soon as she was out of the house, Felicity broke into a run.

The clouds above were heavy as pearls with the coming rain, and she wanted to reach the Lavender Cottage before the world became awash with water. But she was not going to lie to herself—the fresh air and the honest energy of running felt good.

Her heart was still beating fast.

She grew tired very fast, and felt a sharp pain in her side. Felicity smiled bitterly, continuing her way in fast steps. Was it really such an eternity since she used to gaily run around her parents' Somerset house, and with a hoop at that? Not that such exercises were possible for a woman grown, not even according to her mother, who did care about her figure; but no one would have forbidden her to take walks, even in London.

She seemed to have spent too many years in the sickly world of sedan chairs.

Halfway to the cottage, Felicity turned, and looked at the pale edifice of Morwood Hall rising not far in the distance. Life was going on beyond those windows. The Cadogans were, no doubt, still taking tea with the Winterses. Mr. Winters was, most likely, setting his cap on Miss Cadogan, now that the uncomfortable presence of his guest was no more.

He was most likely relieved at the restoration of the decorum, whatever the solicitousness in his eyes.

Felicity swallowed, turned back, and continued on her path toward the cottage.

'You seem to be very worried about the coming rain', Sir Jonathan remarked mildly as he traced the direction of Edmund's gaze.

The direction that led to the window.

It was blasted nonsense. Edmund knew that well. After all, Miss Deacon was probably suffering from nothing more than a moment's indisposition, or even just some unwelcome memory prompted by Miss Cadogan's words.

But he did not want Felicity Deacon to suffer from either.

This protective impulse was no different to what he ordinarily felt toward young women with no husband or father to shield them, Edmund told himself.

On the other hand, he was not sure he was feeling any such impulse toward Priscilla Cadogan right now.

He glimpsed Miss Deacon's figure down in the darkening gardens. It was madcap, but he wanted, for a second only, to run after her. It was a desire as natural as the one that propelled him out of the house and over the fields and wild forest paths, a desire that was the extension of his heart.

'Edmund', his stepmother called his name softly.

At this, the spell was broken. He had guests, he had responsibilities.

He had a bride to win.

Edmund looked back at Sir Jonathan.

'Forgive me my lapse', he said with an effort. 'I only was wondering about the weather'.

Chapter 8

'Oh, I don't know, Miss Deacon', Mrs. Kerr's daughter said doubtfully. 'I sew some things here and there, but I've never made a proper ballgown. I don't know if I can do something with those hoop petticoats, and—'

'Don't worry about that', Felicity replied, sitting at the table in the small farmhouse where the Kerrs now lived.

The house was no hovel—the trade in the shop was probably going well. Felicity even saw some watercolors on the walls.

But one frame—the one Felicity had to turn around to see, and she was not altogether sure it was not placed out of the way on purpose—was empty. Either it was awaiting a pretty picture brought up on the turnpike road from the workshops of Covent Garden, or the picture had recently been sold.

'Don't worry at all', she repeated. 'No one wears hoop petticoats these days but ladies of the court. Natural lines and a short bodice is the order of the day, and, this year, short sleeves'.

'That's good. For you, I mean. You won't have to spend so much on fabric', Jane reasoned. 'But wouldn't it be, oh...a little bit wanton, in the looks of it?'

'Not at all. I suppose— Well, I suppose, the lady who first brought the fashion for these robes over from France was a royal mistress at one point, but years have passed since then. Nowadays, the highest ladies of the land dress this way without incurring any reproach'.

Before yesterday's visit, Felicity's reason for accepting the invitation to the Winterses' ball had been a mix of politeness and curiosity. Now, however, she was quietly enraged to the point of her blood boiling. Devil take Priscilla Cadogan, and she, Felicity, would rather let the devil take her own self than give the heiress any reason to suppose she was hiding from her.

It went against every rule she had learned over these last years. Making an enemy out of the only daughter of the local grandee was not the wisest course of action for anyone, let alone a woman who wanted to be beloved of the *ton* and had neither birth no fortune to achieve it.

But Felicity had once allowed another grandee to run her out of Morwood Hall. She hadn't shown her face there for an eternity as a result. Mr. Winters the elder was dead and cold in his grave, beyond her reach; but the Cadogans were alive and well. She was not going to let them drive her away with their scorn the way he had done.

'I suppose, Miss Deacon', Jane said doubtfully. 'We could do something with that, if only you draw the silhouette for me. What are these gowns usually made of? I don't think mother has any proper silk in her shop'.

'Muslin, most commonly'.

'I don't think she has any Indian muslin, either'. The regret in the young woman's voice was palpable.

'A local one would be perfectly good', Felciity said quickly. 'It's not as though our spinning mules are in any way inferior. Besides, I am going to a country ball, not being presented to Her Majesty'.

'Have you been presented to Her Majesty?' Jane's eyes gleamed with lively curiosity.

Felicity couldn't hope but smile at that. Jane Marsden, nee Kerr, must have thought she was living the life of impossible glamour down in the capital. To her credit, plenty of people far more well-informed thought the same.

'I am afraid not, Mrs. Marsden. I don't have a great lady who could sponsor my presentation. Besides, I doubt there would be much point. Young ladies who go through their debut do so to find fine husbands, and I have little chance of that'.

'Oh, don't say such things, Miss Deacon. You're s–s—well, not exactly pretty', Jane said frankly, 'but so alive, and so well-dressed, and Mother says you know so many things...'

'That last one is not always a good thing in the eyes of some gentle-men'.

'I suppose. My husband's not like that. He never said a word about my borrowing things from the circulating library, as long as they're not novels. He says a clever mother will bring up clever children'.

'That's very reasonable of him'. Felicity thought, unbidden, of Edmund Winters. When he was to marry, his children would be brought up by tutors and governesses. Their mother's knowledge, or the lack of it, would play little role in it. However, he had never been against her borrowing tomes from his father's venerable, unused library, even though sometimes her interest in the matters exceeded his. If Miss Cadogan would one day be struck with the desire to read Pope's translation of *The Iliad*, her husband was unlikely to object.

Priscilla Cadogan would be a happy woman one day, Felicity thought with a sudden yearning, its pain as pulling as a toothache. It's a shame she clearly did not realize it.

'Have you been sewing for a long time, Mrs. Marsden?' Felicity asked to change the subject.

'As long as a I remember. I've always been inventing little things for my younger sisters, and sometimes helping the neighbors with frocks, especially after father opened his shop. But I've never dressed a lady for a ball. That would be a challenge!' The last words were said not with trepidation, but, on the contrary, a kind of anticipation.

'But I suppose you are fairly well-known among the local ladies'. Naturally, someone like Abigail Winters doubtless had a mantua-maker in Bath, if not in London; but someone like, for instance, the local vicar's wife could not possibly afford such extravagance, and Jane was probably a better option than many by far.

'I wouldn't call myself well-known', the woman demurred. 'I just— I just lend a hand, and that's usually with mending rather than a creation from the whole cloth, as it were'.

Felicity smiled at her, likely, an unplanned pun, and Jane hesitated, then smiled in return.

'I could help you', Felicity suddenly said. 'I may not be the literary lioness as some paint me as, but I am, as it were, fairly well-known in some circles, too. I could praise to anyone who would care to listen, be it in Bath or in London itself'.

'Surely you don't mean that'.

'Of course I do!' Suddenly, Felicity found herself annoyed with the world—and with her playing-part in it. She recalled the clever quips of her friends and rivals, sharp political jokes about the Treaty and the war exchanged over a dinner table like darting needles. Here, however, was a woman the very flesh of whose life had been affected by both.

Her husband never quite coming back whole after the war, the crops of their farm never quite selling for any decent price since the signing of the Treaty. She, Felicity, might have fumed at Edmund Winters for dishonoring their affinity years ago, but at least he was doing something to help his tenants. What was Felicity doing but writing down her observations of flowers and bees in the hope it might spur her on to produce yet more verses on improbable, tragic romances?

'I want to help you', Felicity explained. 'I... I want to do something. Something true and particular, and material as the earth under our feet. Would you allow me to help you?'

'Of course. Oh, I'd be so grateful if your plan works."

There was, of course, this little if. If her plan works. If the standing that would have allowed her to execute it would not take a plunge in the next few months—which it might well, if no improbable, tragic romances would be forthcoming.

But Felicity was going to cross this bridge when she came to it.

'I am sure it will', she said firmly, trying to convince herself as much as she did the woman sitting at the table opposite her. 'At least, I am going to do my utmost to make sure it will'.

'It is quite in your fashion', his stepmother observed, 'to be late to the ball in your own house'.

'Forgive me', Edmund said crisply. 'I had to finish writing some letters'.

'Something to do with those oaks?'

'Elms, Mother. The oaks take too long to grow to any useful height, and are therefore unsuited for the purpose'.

'I beg you not to address these words to any woman but me tonight'.

As his gaze roamed the ballroom, Edmund could not help but agree that his stepmother and Miss Deacon succeeded where he would have likely failed (if only, as he sternly reminded himself, because he did not care for the frivolous). Some of the additions around him were doubtless his stepmother's idea—the heavy French girandole, for instance, carrying eight wax candles each. The draperies of dramatic blue velvet that framed the windows for the night were Miss Deacon's notion. He knew it, because he had heard her express it, back on the summer day when the ballroom was empty, and she was flitting about like a dark-haired sprite, talking of Aeolian harps.

The Aeolian harp was there too, of course, a new addition to the salon. This was not the room where most guests tonight were to congregate, and yet, according to Miss Deacon, they were sure to pass it, and take note. Edmund thought it a lot of trouble for very little worth, but rebuffing her advice was somehow beyond his powers. Perhaps, the ties of affection that bound them all those years ago still tethered him to her, together with a more insidious coil of guilt.

Edmund shook his head, stepping forth into the fray. He had little to feel guilt over in that whole affair, had he? These thoughts, they had to be banished for good, especially tonight, when he was supposed to be overawing Miss Cadogan with his hospitality and gallantry.

He could spot her now—an angelic vision of white satin and Spanish silver, waiting demurely with the other ladies.

Miss Deacon, however, he could not see. Perhaps, she was busy, just as he had been? After all, as he could recall from her prodigious output, she was as much of a busy bee as he was himself, with the added factor that, unlike him, she had to work for her bread. She might still be in the Lavender Cottage now, polishing her old lines or inventing new ones.

Before he could finish the thought, however, there was a sound from the doors. Footsteps, the rustling of gowns, curious whispers.

Then, the sea of satin parted, and Edmund saw Felicity Deacon.

She walked fast, without the mincing grace of the daughters of the local gentry; she was taller than them, too, which was obvious now that he saw her among them. And, among the sea of white, she was wearing purple.

No flounces there, no...whatever that lace his stepmother once told him about was called. Calvinist lace? Huguenot lace? There was only the simple and bright expanse of purple, draping itself over her as though she were a Roman matron in her stola, caught beneath her bosom. Her sleeves were short, and the expanse of her creamy-white arms was naked to the eye.

Among the pale daisies of the ballroom, she was an orchid.

He was not the only one to notice that, as was clear. An older man than him started to move in her direction, his intentions clear. The musicians, after all, had just started a lively tune that Edmund himself had learned only recently.

Felicity Deacon did not notice the older man. Smiling, she approached Miss Cadogan, clearly wishing to greet the nigh-only young woman in the ballroom she knew.

In response, Miss Cadogan passed her by, her face studiedly averted, as though they had never met. Or met under circumstances that were best forgotten.

The cut was clear. So was the hurt on Miss Deacon's face.

So was the new hesitation in the older gentleman's steps. It was one thing to desire the acquaintance of a lovely stranger; it was another to approach someone whom the daughter of a great landowner saw fit to cut.

Edmund looked at Priscilla Cadogan, pristine in her white satin, her profile cold; then at Miss Deacon, bright as a flower on fire.

The prudent thing to do would have been to follow the former, the respectable, desirable bride.

But, by God Almighty, would this prudent thing be the right thing, too?

Gritting his teeth, Edmund turned away for Jonathan Cadogan's daughter. Let her find a bridegroom in Hades. Coldness he could forgive, but he could never abide deliberate cruelty.

There was only one salve he could apply to Miss Deacon's unenviable position.

He crossed the room in quick, broad strides, the strides of a man more used to paths than to ballrooms, and reached her.

'Miss Deacon', Edmund raised his voice for all to hear. 'You are truly beautiful tonight. Would you do me the honor of granting me the next dance?'

Felicity Deacon looked shocked. Then her cheeks flushed with delight, and her eyes sparkled like black jewels.

'I would be glad to, especially since it's the very dance I told you about'.

That part was not obvious straightaway, for the strains of music produced by professional musicians, of course, differed greatly from the humming Miss Deacon gave him as an example.

'Moll in the wad'.

'Exactly'. She took his offered arm, and they took their place in the row of couples.

'I have to warn you, Miss Deacon, I did not say I am good at it'.

'It is no problem at all. I am sure you are an apt pupil'.

That way of putting it was very optimistic. Edmund recalled their "lesson" in the empty room weeks ago, and also tried his best to copy the movements of the men around him with more aptitude for fast dances than he had. Miss Deacon, however, was splendid, and it was not only the years of affection—for these were indeed years, as he understood now, the feeling not so much abandoned as buried—that led him to think so. She was sprightly and quick, her silver-stockinged ankles flashing gaily as the hem of her gown rose an inch or two during some particularly daring jump.

'You've saved me', Miss Deacon whispered, her face flushed, as they finished drawing the first star-shaped figure on the floor with their feet. 'Thank you'.

Perhaps, it was the exhilaration of the dance, or the gilded excitement of the evening—or, perhaps, the sheer loveliness of he–r—that prompted Edmund to reply, his voice just as low, "I should have saved you a long time ago."

Her lips parted, and in her eyes flashed the last thing he had expected to see there now.

Fear.

'How do you know I wanted saving? What from?' Her voice was merry. Her voice was trembling.

'From want, of course', Edmund replied, confused. 'From need'.

She spun on her toes, a whirlwind of muslin, and when she turned back to him again, her smile was genuine.

'You should have', Miss Deacon said with brazen ease that would have been startling in anyone else. 'But I forgive you, Mr. Winters'.

He could feel a hundred pairs of eyes upon them, and normally, he would have resented being so watched by people, especially since half the people here he barely knew, and the other half he wished he barely knew. But right now, it seemed strangely right.

A solemn moment requires witnesses, after all.

'Edmund', he said. 'I would be grateful if you could call me Edmund...again'.

They joined hands and slipped down the middle. It was centuries away from the running in the grass they did as children. For one thing, back then they rarely cared about the elegance of the whole movement, but their hands used to be conjoined in just the same way.

'I will do that." Miss Deacon looked breathless, and blooming, and unutterably beautiful. 'Provided you are going to call me Felicity'.

Chapter 9

F elicity awoke late the next morning. In fact, it would have been rather generous to call it morning. The sun was already perilously high in the sky.

She smiled upon her pillow, upon her own momentary self-indulgence and other things. In London, she took pains to cultivate the appearance of silken ease and infinite leisure, but in fact, she usually rose very early, and worked on barely a breakfast.

Now, however, was a special case, she reasoned, and not simply because the ball ended so late into the night.

The world had turned on its axis. Something impossible had happened.

Edmund Winters had chosen her.

Not as a future bride, of course—she was not conceited or deluded enough to think that—but as a dear friend he preferred to the woman he actually was of a mind to make his fiancée only one night past.

They were Edmund and Felicity once more. The laws of time had been overturned.

Still in her nightgown, humming a theatrical tune, Felicity went to another room. Yesterday was the day of the week she usually received her post here. Yesterday was also a day completely consumed by last-minute preparations, and therefore she promised herself to deal with her correspondence later. Infuriatingly, the small business of the day refused to simply evaporate, however enchanting the night, and, sure enough, there was still a small heap of letters lying on the desk.

The top one was from Mr. Flyte. Felicity sighed, guessing at its contents, but even this unwelcome intrusion into her Somerset idyll could not ruin her good mood today.

The one nestling beneath it was much shorter, and thus Felicity unfolded its single sheet first. The handwriting was unknown to her.

Perhaps, it was a note from some literary admirer who found her even in her summer seclusion?

Such letters could be exceedingly silly sometimes, and yet Felicity was a woman of flesh and blood, and she would have lied if she said she was not at the very least a little warmed by them.

She started reading.

Dear Miss Deacon,

I am surprised that you, literary lioness that you are, have decided to abandon your London lair for the depths of Somerset. Such behavior hints either at a sudden change of heart or a less sudden desire for concealment, and, knowing something of your character, I strongly suspect the latter.

Felicity's heart sank. It was one of *those* letters, then. Well, she would have lied, too, if she said it was the first time she received a poison pen.

Due to the circumstances with which you are no doubt familiar, I find myself in Bath. I wonder if you might be curious enough to visit me there. You will find the address in the postscript. I suspect we have more than enough to say to each other.

The letter was signed simply: C. Miles.

Felicity had to sit down. The sunlit day outside might as well have been reigning on another planet.

Claire Miles. After all these years.

Felicity recalled the scene that greeted her in that small withdrawing room in Hampstead. She wished she could bury it forever, but that was impossible. No memory was truly dead, not even if every person featured in it was six feet under.

And Claire Miles, it seems, was still very much walking the earth.

Explaining to Mrs. Winters that she was going to go to Bath for a day or two was not a difficult thing. In fact, the older woman told her, she was surprised Miss Deacon had not done so sooner. After all, a worldly creature like her must have been bored in the green quietude of their lands, and hungering for the excitement of the town.

Excitement. Felicity smiled at that, and her smile was brittle. Perhaps, that was one word to describe what she felt.

The streets of Bath were gaiety and satin and sedan chairs, as always. This was, after all, what the fashionable circles called the Season, and not everyone could afford a turn in London. Besides, ladies and gentlemen of ample means and frail health enjoyed the waters and the card parties of this place, as usual.

But theirs was not the world Felicity was aiming for. Not today, at any rate.

The address Claire Miles had given her was noticeably far from the good inn where Felicity stayed, even in terms purely geographical. In terms of the means and the circumstances, the place was galaxies away. Felicity regretted that she had no habit to perfume her handkerchiefs, for the smell in the street was decidedly unwholesome.

In London terms, this was not quite St. Giles, but certainly a rookery a good number of steps below Russel Square.

The house that corresponded to the address and the description had clearly once been a city mansion of some local grandee, built before Bath attracted the royal attention, and with it the noble and the moneyed clientele from far away. Felicity wouldn't have been surprised if someone told her that royalists used to gather here in the days of Oliver Cromwell, in a world more violent than that Robert Adam ever knew.

Those days were long past, however, and the glory of the address with them. Now, the house was clearly subdivided into rooms to let, and, judging by the gray laundry hanging out on the windowsills to dry, not to mention the smell, ran rather sloppily.

Gingerly, Felicity walked through the door. No one prevented her from doing so. She might have well been coming to murder Claire Miles in her bed, for all they knew.

There was a brief period in her life when she and her mother lived in a place like this, if not for long. Felicity had been as eager as her mother was to climb out of there. She accepted the cup willingly, and had no one to blame for forcing the contents down her throat.

It was only that she did not know how deep the cup would be, how bitter the dregs.

Flimsy doors responded to her touch, parting easily like meat to the contact with a sharp knife. In some rooms, she saw nothing but emptiness and some meager furniture—here the former ballroom with fine plaster peeling off the walls, here what used to be a withdrawing room, now a home to a bed and a child's cot. Sometimes, she saw faces looking back at her—not so much indignant as curious, or simply numbly tired.

The ground floor, the first, the second. A sordid pilgrim's progress. No sign of Claire Miles.

There was only one flight of stairs left. One that led to the attic.

Felicity hesitated before it. Partly it was mere disbelief. Was that woman really in such dire straits right now that she could only afford the cheapest room, even in a place such as this? She used to be a veritable toast of the town. Perhaps, she, Felicity, had simply missed something during her search below.

Partly, it was a simple, animal fear. She had always been afraid of dark spaces, of the basements and the attics, where old ghosts lurked.

But sooner or later, one had to face them. If she turned and fled now, the ghost would still be there, its shroud whispering secrets.

Felicity took a deep breath, and ascended the stairs.

In the days gone by, the attic must have been where the maids of the house slept. It had not undergone much change in the centuries that passed since, even though some of the damp decay that was set in the rest of the house could be felt in the air now.

The woman who had written the letter that surprised Felicity and sucked the joy out of the summer day was standing in the middle of the room. Claire Miles was not tall—had never been tall—but there was something imposing in her presence nonetheless. She was wearing an old, but incongruously expensive gown of gentle lilac color, as though she were still the literary equivalent of a debutante, a 'girl genius', a brilliant protege.

Felicity did not need to inspect the stack of books piled up on the bedside table. She had read most of them, back when her own star was not quite in ascendancy and she wanted to study the works of those she thought her betters.

She knew Miss Miles was the author of every single tome, every single poetic anthology kept here.

'Miss Deacon', the older woman greeted her. 'You look wonderful. But then, you always have. I see you no longer wear gowns that bare your ankles?'

'I am not an adolescent anymore. Only girls who have not yet come of age wear such short skirts'.

'Don't be so hard on yourself. Courtesans wear them, too. I would have offered you to sit down, only there is only one chair here'. With this, Claire Miles sat in it, as though she were a schoolmistress, and Felicity the troublemaker in front of her.

'Why have you called me here?' Felicity asked.

'To inform you of something, Miss Deacon. You have been flaunting your sins too publicly, and, at my word, they might become very public indeed'.

'I have no notion what it is you are speaking about'.

'I know about your yearly sojourn in a certain seaside town. I know its reason. I know your companion'.

'You know nothing'.

'I know more than you can imagine. I might not have much money no–w—never have, not even in the best of times—but I still have connections. Not to mention I have eyes and ears of my own, and a working brain, too. I have it all here." She tapped on her forehead. 'Names, times, dates. The scandal sheets are going to be absolutely thrilled to hear them all'.

'I highly doubt that', Felicity said as lightly as she could, which was not much. 'I am no heiress, no grande dame. My comings and goings are not of interest to many'.

'Of course you are no grande dame. If you were, people would have been simply thrilled by thes–e...comings and goings. The *ton* lives according to its own laws. Especially those ladies belonging to it who are both rich and married. But you are neither, Miss Deacon. You are living on the edge of ruin. I know that, because so did I, once. I can guarantee, there are already people wondering just how autobiographical your poems about passionate, flesh-killing passion are'.

'That is a flimsy base for any construction'.

'Once they know what I do, it is going to be flimsy no longer'.

'What do you want from me?'

'I want money'.

At this, Felicity laughed.

'All this Gothic display, and for such a tawdry goal! Oh, Miss Miles, it is a wonder you went out of fashion. You always knew how to create an atmosphere'.

At this taunting, Miss Miles' expression became a mask of rage.

'You know very well why I 'went out of fashion', you lightskirt. You were there. You were the instrument of that'.

'I was nothing of the kind. I was simply another bauble to interest your patron'.

'Tell that to someone utterly stupid. I know a flirt when I see one, and I certainly know a schemer'.

Oh, there was a schemer in that story. Except it was not me.

'I don't have ready money now'.

'I am a patient woman, Miss Deacon. I can wait'.

Chapter 10

When Felicity finally arrived home, she sat at the desk without changing, her light summer coat still buttoned tightly against her chest. She had had hours of the journey to think on what had just happened, of the danger now hanging over her.

Claire Miles. God, she was sure the woman was long since dead, or abroad, or simply— Simply dissolved in the teeming masses of people in the capital where she had once made her career.

Her all-too-brief career.

Felicity's own career, of course, could turn out to be just as brief. Especially if she didn't pay.

She raised her eyes, gazing out into the garden, the green grounds, the faint white of Morwood Hall glowing on the summer's day somewhere beyond. It was so close—so seemingly close-but the distance between her and that house might as well have been the miles between distant stars, right now.

Felicity imagined, for a second, rising from her desk, walking to the home of her patroness—to Edmund's house—explaining what happened, asking for help.

Telling the truth.

But, God, what an ugly truth it was going to be. Too ugly for the Axminster carpet of their lovely withdrawing room.

She was going to be thrown out of the place like a misbehaving cur. Or, rather, politely escorted out. For the second time in her life; and, this time, there would be no miraculous return.

Shaking her head, Felicity lowered her eyes once again. No, that was not the solution. If there was a way to raise money to pay the blackmailer, she was going to have to accomplish that on her own.

Perhaps, it was the necessity gripping her throat, or, perhaps, the old exhaustion, but the ideas refused to come. Her imagination might as well have been a plain of scorched earth left once the marauding armies had departed.

Felicity closed her eyes. There should have been a way to free her from that grasp. To calm her nerves and relax her limbs, if nothing else.

A thought struck. She was quite sure that she had just this kind of solution among the things she took with her when she came to Morwood Hall in the first place.

Strictly speaking, it was a medicine for a cold. Felicity knew she was rather prone to throat aches even during the hot summer months, and took some with her just in case. But it contained enough laudanum for it to work.

Felicity poured herself a glass of water, and measured a few dark-colored drops out of the small bottle. Then, thinking better of it, she added a couple more drops to the liquid.

And one more, just to be sure.

Edmund could not quite wait for Miss Deacon to come back from her sojourn to the circulating libraries of Bath. At least, he had assumed those were her primary destination. The few days she had remained in the city of the healing waters could not have been enough to participate in any sort of social entertainments.

He told himself such hurry is unseemly, as he walked down the garden path. After all, it might well be Miss Deacon's hasty departure after the ball was precipitated specifically by his forwardness during.

But, his inner voice murmured, it might not have been.

Edmund Winters found himself nervous as a schoolboy around his first infatuation. He would have said so, at least, had he not realized that, as an actual schoolboy, he had never suffered from infatuations of any sort. There was the intense friendship with Miss Deacon, back then a simple Felicity; then there was a long period of nothing but talk, the usual adolescent talk of boys who thought they knew more about ladies than they actually did; then the staid, slow courtship of Miss Cadogan.

But that courtship was now over for good. Even if Priscilla Cadogan herself could forgive a man who snubbed her during a ball where she was supposed to be an unofficial guest of honor, her father never would.

Now, the only road in front of him led to Felicity Deacon's door, and Edmund had never felt gladder before, and never before had his step been lighter.

She did not open immediately. When she did, he saw she was still dressed in her morning garments, despite the sun being already high in the sky.

'Miss Deacon, I've heard you have come back from Bath...'

She smiled a strange, dreamy smile.

'So I have'.

'May I come in?'

Miss Deacon took a pause before answering. When she looked into his eyes, Edmund was momentarily entranced by her glittering, dark gaze. Until he noticed that her pupils were wider than ever before.

'Miss Deacon', Edmund asked cautiously. 'Are you quite well?'

'Never better." She giggled. 'Oh, I feel so...light'.

'Have you been suffering from a toothache?'

'What?'

'I have seen the effect of laudanum before, Miss Deacon. My mother's teeth ache often, as does her head. It's the remedy she prefers. Besides, there is quite a lot of the concoction in the tonics against the cold'.

'Oh'. Felicity Deacon turned around several times, as though she were a star moving around her orbit. 'No, not a toothache. Just...a heartache, I suppose'.

'I could summon our family physician', Edmund said, feeling more and more awkward with every passing second.

At this, Miss Deacon laughed, and her laughter was like sparks dancing in the air.

'I don't need a physician, Edmund', she replied, calling him by his Christian name no–w—the name she had not used since they were both children. 'Besides, you have promised to call me Felicity from now on'.

'You remember that'.

'Of course I do', she said with quiet tenderness. 'How can I not?'

He took a step toward her, wanting, for a second, nothing so much as to take her hand between his, and feel the beating of her heart in her wrist.

'Felicity...'

'Edmund, I don't know what to do'.

'What happened?'

'I cannot tell you'.

'Please, do', he urged her. 'I cannot imagine there is anything I cannot help you with'.

'You would not want to help me, if you knew the truth'. Felicity stumbled in her half-conscious rotations, and Edmund caught her without thinking.

'I cannot imagine that. Unless you have been secretly hunting people in the rookeries of London'.

'Edmund Winters, have you just made a joke?'

'It seems so'. Edmund smiled, despite feeling more and more disturbed with every second.

'I am a bad influence on you'.

'A benevolent one, you mean'.

She shook her head, slowly, as though she were moving underwater, drifting away from him.

'Do you know what might help me?'

'What?'

'If I never have to go back'.

'To London?'

'To Margate'.

'Margate? The seaside resort?' Edmund was perplexed. What on earth would she be doing in Margate, especially against her will?

Felicity nodded.

'I don't want to. I cannot do this anymore'.

'No one is going to force you', Edmund spoke heatedly. He had very little idea of what she was talking about. He sensed something profoundly wrong, however; a dead body under the calm surface of a lake, a ghost in the dark.

'They will, Edmund. They will'.

'Who are they, Felicity?' he urged her. 'Tell me'.

But she said nothing. It was as though something changed in her in a trice, and the dreamy exuberance morphed into a sullen, complete lack of spirit. Edmund remained with her for a while. Then she simply wandered away through the rooms, as though he were not there, and lay upon the sofa, gazing into the empty air in a kind of stupor.

By then, Edmund had already taken the decision it was time for him to do some traveling of his own.

Chapter 11

When Felicity opened her eyes, her throat was dry, and the world beyond the window was the faint gray of early morning.

She felt rather supine, and continued lying there until the golden scythe of dawn cut through the clouds. Then, massaging the vision into the status of a sign from above, Felicity made an effort and staggered from the sofa down to the desk where the flagon of water was still standing. She poured herself some, splashing some onto the front of her morning gown. When did she change? The memories of what she had done while in the pleasant half-dreaming state were hazy. Well, she must have changed at some point during those long hours, otherwise she would not be wearing the gown now.

The irrefutable logic of that statement bolstered Felicity's confidence in her power of thinking returning for good, and she drank some more water. Then she retrieved a thin linen towel from another room, and pressed it against the soaked front of her dress; as she did so, the embarrassment over the water stains grew as her consciousness was fully returning. She looked over the assortment of papers upon her desk. A flicker of hope surged in her chest. This was the whole reason she took laudanum, wasn't it?

Felicity sat down to read her own writing. After a few minutes, her heart sank. This was indeed quite a lot of new lines, but none of them were fit even for reworking, much less publication. Not because the imagery was dull or the meter ill-use–d—she had mastered both well enough to make use of them even in the haze. But the subjects of that imagery... Just reading them made Felicity's head spin anew. It was not unlike walking through some malicious house of mirrors, the reality distorted.

Screaming walls, dark moors, monsters under the bed.

She could not use that. She was known for a very particular kind of poetry. Risqué, yes; some suggestive imagery, yes; but otherwise smooth as glass, maidens in flower crowns languishing for dark suitors.

This would not do. No, this would not do at all.

Felicity felt, for a second, like lowering her head upon her hands and weeping.

Her gaze roamed over the room. Something here was not quite right.

The source of her disquiet turned out to be a foreign object—a small note lying on the desk. She seized upon it and read it.

Dear Felicity,

I have found you decidedly unwell, and I hope you are feeling better now...

Felicity's cheeks lit up. Edmund had been here? In the Lavender Cottage? He saw her...intoxicated?

But of course, she realized. She woke up under a blanket, after all. Felicity had never been considering enough for herself even when sober and hale to stop and pick a blanket up to make herself more comfortable.

But Edmund was. For all his stiff ways, for all his past sins.

I am afraid certain matters of business are going to take me away from Morwood Hall for a week or more. I am very sorry that I cannot be by your side in your hour of need. I hope to rectify that once I am back.

I hope to see you more often then. I hope you share this wish of mine.

I hope you have woken up feeling better.

The letter was not signed, which was strange for a man of Edmund's meticulousness.

Fear gripped her. What had prompted this decision? What had she done in her delirium?

What had she told him?

What if she confessed her secret? Her entire sordid double life?

If she did, Felicity tried to tell herself, Edmund would not have been leaving her courteous notes. The only message he would have left for her would have been an order to get out and never approach the lands around Morwood Hall again.

But that could not have been that far in the future.

It was like a nightmare unfolding in front of her very eyes, the fabric of reality unraveling.

Felicity thought of her mother's imperatives, the lusts of the older man who is holding her future in his hands. She had gotten used to it, numb to it. She had heard sailors traveling in the far northern countries growing similarly numb to the cold around them, as though their bodies morphed into ice. Is that what had happened to her, bit by bit, inch by inch, over those last few years in London?

Well, evidently not completely, her inner voice whispered. *If you are so hardened and immune to pain, after all, why is it that you cannot write anymore?*

She recalled her last conversation with Mr. Flyte, that last day in Margate. Plenty of reasonable men would have said that he was merely laying bare what was unspoken before. Besides, what did she expect? When you sell your body for puffs in gazettes, what on earth can you expect but the ceasing of the latter if you stop doing so?

But he didn't have to go as far as he did. He didn't have to threaten to pull the strings to make sure the praise for her work dried up in other corners, too.

"You would do that to me anyway once you are tired of me," she had said then, bitter and desperate. "That is what happened to Claire Miles, isn't it? Isn't it?"

"Maybe." He had shrugged his shoulders, barely even losing his kindly avuncular appearance. "But I am not tired of you yet."

Edmund had never been to Margate before.

It was not that his family had been indifferent to the newly hailed pleasures of the seaside. When his parents wanted to partake of the healthy sea air, however, they chose the blue-blooded Brighton for their trip, with its fine pavilions and illustrious guests. No one could accuse them of a lack of ambition.

Margate was a more modest place, however, and lodgings offered to the travelers did not resemble Gargantuan artifacts from some fallen empire. On the other hand, they were much more numerous than anything Edmund had seen in Brighton.

His quest was deceptively simple. Walking into one, talking to the owner or owners, asking them if they had seen a lady of a certain description stay here in the year past, and move on to the next.

The plan was quite madcap, and Edmund realized that already after the second boarding house he visited.

Just how many dark-haired young women, to think of it, have stayed in this popular seaside town since, say, last spring? To him, Felicity, with her heavy black hair and her haunted dark eyes, was a singular creature, something made of quicksilver. To them, howeve–r—the tired men and women who took care of well-worn room–s—she would have been just another traveling miss, come to relax among the healthful salty air and the circulating libraries.

Edmund's senses were telling him to spend a night in one of the least suspicious lodgings from the number of those he visited, and turn back tomorrow. There was nothing for him here but a whisper of a woman who had taken too much laudanum. It might well have been that she was simply recalling some unfortunate childhood holiday, space and time collapsing in her head, the years rolling back like a carpet.

They will, Edmund. They will.

She might have been referencing her parents, in those days when both were still alive, Edmund tried to reason with himself. After all, what were the chances that she, a real-life woman of flesh and blood, was a victim of some malicious conspiracy as though she were a heroine of some Gothic novel?

But the chance was there. It was puny and pale, but it was there, and it was impossible to ignore.

This inn looked as though it had been standing on the farther reaches of Margate since the days of Queen Anne, if not Queen Bess.

It was certainly not the kind of place where a woman of means and a taste for life in the light of others' glances would choose to stay.

Nonetheless, Edmund went in.

'A pretty brunette above twenty?' the proprietor asked as doubtfully as at least a dozen of proprietors had asked before him on that rapidly fading day. 'Those words fit plenty of ladies'.

'The woman in question has rather unusual eyes. Very dark, almost black'.

'Hm. There might have been someone. Honey', he called into the other room.

A plump woman entered, holding a book of household ledgers under her arm.

'Honey', the owner repeated, 'this gentleman wants to know about one of our guests. There was a dark-eyed lady here, I think? You couldn't talk enough about her'.

'Well, of course I couldn't! Say what you want, but we're a respectable place, and it's not as though I am stupid. Her wedding ring was cheap, though she was all dressed as if for Almack's. Must've been bought quickly, just to make her look decent. But if you ask me—'

'I'm not', her husband said quickly.

'I am', Edmund interjected. 'The woman I am looking for is not married. But if you think that your guest hadn't been a true married woman, either...' A sickeningly sordid picture started coalescing in his mind.

'She wasn't'.

'Was she alone?'

He knew the answer. Of course he knew the answer. What other answer could there be? Young women didn't buy themselves marriage rings for marriages that never were just to stay in seaside resorts alone or with their mothers for company.

The answer came like a downward swing of a sword.

'No, there was a gentleman with her. They called themselves Mr. and Mrs. Flyte'.

Chapter 12

The light filtered through the leaves of oaks looked different than when it was unfettered.

Felicity raised her head and closed her eyes, allowing the shadowed, dappled light to touch her face.

She knew, deep down, that she was living on borrowed time. The realization of that had strangled the last shred of willingness to write from her.

Nonetheless, she could not help but marvel at the small miracles of nature, at the wide acres and the forests of silver-green. She tried her best to banish from her mind the realization that she is going to leave these acres and these forests behind soon enough, this time never to return.

She tried to...

'Miss Deacon', a familiar voice sounded softly behind her, and she turned, the magic extinguished.

Felicity's heart beat faster—not with some lovesickness, for sure, but with dread. The anticipation of a scaffold, which was at times worse than the moment when the blade parted your life from you.

Stop this, she silently ordered herself. *You still don't know for sure. Edmund might have genuinely had things to attend to. Something to do with the estate, perhaps.*

Maybe something to do with his elms.

But the fact that he had reverted to the ceremonious Miss Deacon did not speak in support of this notion.

'Edmund', Felicity replied, refusing to bow down to this retracing of steps. 'How was your journey?'

'It was eventful'.

He looked as though he had just got out of the carriage. His hair was mussed, his eyes sleepless as the eyes of a man tossing and turning in hired beds would be.

Worst of all, he was looking at herwith... No, not with disgust. Not even with disappointment.

He was looking at her as though he was seeing her for the last time before her transportation to the place of execution, and wanted to imbibe her whole being with his eyes.

Because he knew he was never going to see her again.

She decided to be the one to let the axe fall.

'Where did you go?'

A hesitation. The golden twilight reflecting in his eyes.

'Margate'.

'I see'.

'Do you?'

Felicity took a step closer.

'I know you did not go there for the seaside air', she said quietly. 'And you have told Mrs. Winters that your trip was to Bath'.

'You know that, too'. A kind of resigned tenderness.

'I usually do take care to find out as much as I can about things happening around me'.

'Then you cannot fault me for doing the same'.

'No, I suppose not. I was a fool, taking more of the laudanum than is advisable'.

'I am sorry. I should not have seen you like that'.

'But if you had not, you would not have found out what I truly am. So, why the regrets?' She smiled, quickly and bitterly.

'For this precise reason, Miss Deacon. Felicity. Tell me...have you and Mr. Flyte been in an improper kind of relationship?'

'Are you asking me if I am his mistress? I suppose the answer is yes. Except...'

'Except?'

'It is more complicated than that'.

'Tell me, then'. A kind of urgency. A kind of yearning. 'Have you been unwilling? You've said—'

'Of course I was unwilling, Edmund. He is old enough to be my father, and... I know your father had been older than your stepmother, too, but that is different. Or, at least, I dearly hope that is different. Mrs. Winters was a noble-born young woman with an iron wall of protection around her. A dowry. Prospects. I had none of this after my father's death'.

'Did Mr. Flyte promise you literary fame? There, in the beginning?'

'Mr. Flyte promised me that I wouldn't starve. Or, rather, he promised my mother that we wouldn't. He knew, after all, that he would have to get her blessing. It would not do for a girl as inexperienced as myself to arrange trysts behind her back. I might get caught, after all'.

'You were sixteen'.

'Almost seventeen. I was unwilling at first, but mother had –a-a rather frank conversation with me. She told me that my hopes of forging my way in the world of letters all by myself was foolish, while Mr. Flyte was going to give me connections and assistance and endless puffing in his paper. That, now that father was gone, and I had no hope of a good marriage anymore, after your and your father's decision, I had to support my family by other means'.

'Your family meaning her'.

'Well, it was not as though I myself wanted to starve. I did not want to surrender at first. I was rather foolishly defiant. I did not want to accept that there was only one coin in which a woman can pay for success in this world'.

'Surely not the only one'.

'The only one that I could find in my purse, then'.

Felicity thought back to that first year after her career was launched, seemingly a blazing comet appearing out of nowhere. The acclaim and the invitations, and the trouble sleeping. Not because her guilty conscience troubled her after such a sinful fall—although she knew that was the way moral guardians would have had it—but the curious sensation of her body not being quite hers anymore. It was as though someone cut the threads tethering her true self to it with a knife.

Edmund raised his hand, and she flinched, every particle of her flesh expecting violence. Instead, he touched her temple, and his fingers drew a wandering line down the side of her face.

It was the first time he had touched her like this. Felicity shivered pleasantly under the warmth of his hand.

It was also likely to be the last, and she knew it.

'Who is Claire Miles?' he asked. 'I recall your reaction when the Cadogans mentioned her. Another poetess from Mr. Flyte's list?'

'You are courteous as ever, Edmund. Another man would have said another filly from his stable, and would have been equally right. She was another adolescent genius, another bright comet, one from a decade ago. She burned down like Icarus, some said. Just—disappeared. They did not know the story behind it was too sordid to bear any resemblance to the Greek gods'.

'I would not say so. The dealings of the Greek gods with mortal women were often as sordid as it comes'.

'I thought you did not read your Ovid'.

'I did. Recently'.

Her heart twinged at the thought.

'After the ball?'

'Before it. Two weeks after your arrival'.

'Miss Miles had been ruined by nothing but her patron's desire for someone new, but she blamed me wholeheartedly. I suppose, she was not completely wrong. I looked rather down upon her then, with pity. I even thought my taking her place was going to free her. I did not know it was only going to free her into a free fall. I should have guessed'.

'I imagine she would have had good savings, if her fame was anything like yours'.

'If it were anything like mine, she would have had nothing. Or almost nothing. I can bet the gown upon my back that she first came to him as poor and unadorned as I did, and just as willing to agree to any conditions and sign any atrocious contract for a chance at an income. I was paid a pittance, while he kept a fine gig and plans to buy a modest country house in Somerset'.

'Do you mean he has not only been taking advantage of you, but stealing from you?' The expression on Edmund's face was almost incredulous. It was as if he could not believe that such low skullduggery could exist in the world. Although, why as if? He had been brought up in the straitlaced and genteel world of the gentry—away from the realm of cutthroat commerce his father had once inhabited, not quite in the dissolute echelons of high aristocracy. The height of dishonorable behavior he must have witnessed so far must have been a man too tardy to marry his compromised sweetheart.

'It is hardly stealing. Show our correspondence to any court of law, and they are going to say that my mentor has only been taking what was due to him; that he had been, if anything, too generous with the flighty slip of a girl that I am'.

'Hardly—'

'No', Felicity cut him off. 'Believe me, I have rued my naiveté many a time. I have thought of extricating himself this way and that. There is no legal way to do that'.

'I am sure there is. If there is, I am going to find it'.

Felicity stared at him, dumbfounded. A faint hope flickered in her heart. Was it possible that miracles did happen? That her life was not a bleak cavern after all?

'You...you are not disgusted with me?'

'I am disgusted with the people who dishonored and despoiled a child'.

'Hardly a child. Some girls already marry at the age I was back then'.

'Yes. And some do not'.

'Does it mean...' Felicity swallowed. 'That I can...stay?'

'Of course you can stay. You are my stepmother's honored guest, after all'.

And, just like that, the fire-flicker of hope had been snuffed out.

'An honored guest. Of course'.

'Felicity. Miss Deacon', he corrected himself hastily. 'I hope you understand... That is, I am sure you understand why I cannot court you now. Why I cannot think of making you my wife'.

'Because I am a wanton, disorderly creature'.

'Because there will be talk. Felicity, I... If it had been merely your station in life, your need to earn your bread, I would have disregarded it all. I promise, I would have. But what you have told m–e—if there are rumors, and Mr. Flyte does not seem the kind of man to keep his tongue behind his teeth when pressured...'

'I imagine invitations to good houses would dry up rather quickly, yes'. Felicity could not quite keep a touch of bitterness from her voice. Her self-control had never been perfect, and now it was, if anything, run rugged.

'Everything my father has built, everything he had dedicated his life to...'

'Your father's shadow again. I can almost see it here on the forest floor, stretching between us'.

'Felicity. I beg you to understand. I am going to help you as much as I can. I won't leave you trapped in this horror'. Edmund Winters turned away, and took a few steps.

Fresh leaves were soft under his feet, and made not a sound.

Felicity stared at him, at his figure outlined in the golden glow of the setting sun, made all the darker by the light.

He paused on the edge of the clearing. He turned his head back to her, as though pulled by some invisible thread.

'I beg you to understand', Edmund repeated, his voice pained. 'There are some things a gentleman simply cannot do'.

The room in Felicity's inn was filled with her heavy trunks. She stared at them, feeling a belated guilt over abandoning Mrs. Winters' hospitality so abruptly. The kindly woman, after all, had little notion of what passed between Felicity and her stepson, and no notion at all of the reason for its ending. If Felicity was so set on leaving Morwood Hall then and there, she should have... No, not explained to Mrs. Winters the truth, perhaps, but at least invented a polite and plausible lie.

It was too late for that now. The only thing Felicity could do was to write a letter.

The only thing she now had the ability to write, it seemed like.

She closed her eyes for a second. Claire. Mr. Flyte. Her mother. As soon as they realized that they had squeezed her dry, they were going to pounce on her like wild cheetahs.

She could show none of this, of course. As far as Mrs. Winters was to be concerned, she, Felicity, had merely left Morwood Hall so abruptly because of her poor aging mother's health, and she had left it for the settled prosperity awaiting her in the capital.

She sighed, and put pen to paper.

Chapter 13

E dmund's logic was simple.

If Mr. Flyte was looking to buy a small country house in Somerset, it stood to reason that he would cultivate the acquaintance of local grandees. It might even be that one of them might know who exactly did the newspaper proprietor borrow the money for the house from.

That he had indeed borrowed from somewhere, Edmund had not a shadow of a doubt. He knew something of that world, the churn and the dregs of finance, if only because his father had been born and bred there. He knew that practically no man of fashion, be he a journalist or a duke, lived according to his means, and avoided debt entirely.

Indeed, that was one of the reasons he, Edmund, had always avoided the world in question. The depth of the countryside might not have been without its deprivations and cruelties, but it lacked this deceptiveness of a soap-bubble surface.

That is, he had avoided it until today. Now, he had little choice.

Or, rather, there had been a kind of a choic–e—abandon Miss Deacon to her doom or do something morally unpleasant to get her out.

To him, it was no choice at all.

'I have to commend your bravery, I suppose, Mr. Winters', Sir Jonathan told Edmund, as the latter was admitted to the withdrawing room. 'Most men would not have dared to call upon the man whose daughter they had spurned publicly'.

'I would have apologized for that, Sir Jonathan, had I regretted it for a second. Your daughter had treated my guest with undeserved cruelty'.

'Your guest, is it? People are calling her otherwise'.

'People would have little cause to do so, soon enough. Miss Deacon departed Morwood Hall yesterday. She is very unlikely to return'.

'I see. I do hope you have not come here to attempt to renew your courtship of Priscilla. I am sure that whatever measure of sense your father had passed down to you would tell you that that is a hopeless venture'.

'With all due respect, Sir Jonathan, that is not what I have come here for'.

'No? I am all ears'.

'Is the name of Mr. Anthony Flyte familiar to you?'

'Great God, Mr. Winters, how on earth do you know such a man as that?'

'I suppose the answer to my question is yes'.

'It is, but I am rather curious. He is notably below you in every way there is'.

That must have been quite something for Sir Jonathan Cadogan to admit, that there was indeed someone on earth below the young man he thought to be so unworthy of his daughter.

But right now, Edmund was not in the mood or the place to ponder the intricacies of Sir Jonathan's psyche.

'He has been threatening a friend of mine'.

'How on earth did he gain leverage upon a man of your circle?'

'I have different people in my circle'.

'It seems our circles must be much more different than I had ever suspected. Much different indeed'.

'I suppose. I know that Mr. Flyte had been recently borrowing money for a house in Somerset. I wonder if you happen to know the name of the one—or those—he is indebted to'.

'I might. Shameful as it for me to admit, me and the man you are talking about might have shared one or two creditors in the past'.

Edmund must have stared noticeably, for Sir Jonathan replied not without some irritation,

'Don't look at me so, Mr. Winters. You are a young man still, and childless. Educating a son is a great expense, and bringing a daughter out is not a cheap undertaking, either'.

But Edmund could not quite stop thinking—so, that was what the old-fashioned magnificence of Sir Jonathan's household rested upon. His feudal hospitality of which he was so proud had been as dependent on the exchange of cash under an interest rate as any sea voyage or another mercantile endeavor that the Cadogans would have openly despised.

'Could you give me the name of those creditors?'

'What are you intending?'

'It's quite simple, really. I am planning to buy Mr. Flyte's debts from him'.

'All for the sake of revenge for that friend of yours?'

'Not revenge." Edmund shook his head. 'I am not hot-blooded enough for revenge. Insurance'.

'They are likely to demand great sums for those great debts'.

'Then I am going to pay them great sums'.

Felicity knew what to expect when she crept in back home like a thief. Surely enough, her mother greeted her with her arms folded across her chest, and her expression that of a statue made of stone.

'May I ask what are you doing here?' Mary Deacon asked her daughter, eyebrows raised.

'There were complications. I had to cut my visit to Morwood Hall short, and—'

'You have made a mess of things once again'. It was a statement, as definite and final as the last sentence of a judge.

'It wasn't my fault." Felicity found herself being forced into a defensive position, her voice thinning to the tinny sound of her childhood. 'Mr. Winters found out about my—about the arrangements we have made with Mr. Flyte, and...' God, there was so much she had not told her. For good reason. She did not want whatever tentative understanding had been blossoming between her and her childhood friend to be sullied by her mother's interpretation, even via letters. 'He gave me to understand that he would like to cease our courtship'.

The blow came without warning, like a thunderbolt from a clear sky. One second, Felicity was standing unbent; the next, she was clutching her flaming cheek, skin stinging.

'You have acted like a fool, in other words. A courtship! You could have been a gentry bride by now, then, our position assured. And it was all ruined because of your inability to keep your secrets?'

'He knew about Margate, Mother. He found out about that'.

'Then you should have denied it all. Heavens above, do you not have a crumb of womanly wit in your head, Felicity?'

'It looks like I don't', Felicity replied quietly.

'Have you at least written something while in Somerset?'

Felicity thought of Claire Miles, and how unlikely she was to be paid what she demanded now. A kind of doomed glee rose in her heart. It was the feeling of a man going down with a sinking ship, but knowing that his enemies were going to end up with Davy Jones just as he himself was. At least, once Claire sent her no doubt luridly embroidered story to the papers, while she, Felicity, was going to end up in a workhouse or worse, her mother was very unlikely to fare much better. The public was not kind to fallen women; but it did not love ladies who pushed their unmarried daughters into men's beds for their own gain, either.

'I am working on something'.

'In other words, you have not finished anything'.

'No, Mother. I have not'.

'What am I to do with you?' Mary Deacon sighed. Her features softened, and she looked, for a second, very much like the sweet and tired mother of a too-wild offspring whom she thought herself to be. It was like a glimpse into a past that never was, but where one would have dearly liked to return.

That was the reason Felicity offered her a reassuring smile, or at least tried to.

She did not succeed.

Chapter 14

The letter was not the easiest to write. It was not every day that Edmund Winters found himself threatening proprietors of literary newspapers. Or anyone.

But that day, it was as though something unseen had steeled his resolve and propelled him down the lines.

To Mr. Anthony Flyte,

I trust this letter finds you in good health. It is most likely that you do not know my name. I am, however, extremely well-acquainted with yours. I am also well-acquainted with your plans, with your prosperity of the last years, and with the means with which you had achieved this prosperity. Moreover, I know the men you borrowed money from. I imagine you would be rather shocked by my frank reference to such transactions. There is no need. As any man of property in our corner of Somerset would tell you, my father earned his fortune in the world of commerce instead of inheriting it from the previous generation as, according to their opinion, a gentleman ought to do. I have always considered myself my father's son, if not always in this aspect.

Both men you have arranged your loans from have recently agreed to allow me to buy your debts. I have all the papers confirming it, and I can call in the debts in question any day, which is what I am planning to do unless we come to an agreement.

I do not want your money, for I have my own. I also have no literary ambitions, and anyhow I don't think I could satisfy the main requirements of what you are looking for from those you make into lions of the letters: namely, being young, vulnerable, and female. The only thing I am going to demand of you—for, make no mistake, it is indeed a demand—is justice.

I know of the nature of the unofficial agreement between yourself and Miss Felicity Deacon. You are going to release her from the agreement in question on the day this letter reaches you, and not a week later. You are also going to pay her the sums you neglected to pay her for all the years when she made your fortune. For she had indeed made your fortune. I foresee your arguments. First of all, it is a great sum. I am sure it is; I would even argue that is rather the point. Second, the financial affairs of several years are always hard to disentangle. If so, I can lend you the services of my steward. I cannot promise that the results are going to be pleasing to you, but they will be accurate.

At this point, you would likely ask if I am quite finished with my requests. My answer would be that I am not. I know about a young lady by the name of Claire Miles. I know what happened to her, and what had made her take up the unfortunate trade of blackmail. You stood at the roots of her misery, even though she blames someone else for it. It would be only fair and just if you remedy it. I understand that, after you have fulfilled your financial obligations to Miss Deacon, conferring a decent pension on Miss Miles might be difficult. But it is not going to be as difficult as it will be if I call in your debts, which I am going to do should you fail to fulfill any of my demands.

For, make no mistake, these are indeed demands.
Best wishes,
Mr. Edmund Winters of Morwood Hall, Somerset.

Edmund's heart was beating fast—one would have said, as though in the heat of a duel, except he had never fought a duel in his whole scrupulous, scandal-free life.

He heard soft footsteps of a lady entering the room, and turned his head. Perhaps, too quickly, too hopefully. He knew of Miss Deacon's flight, and knew that he was most unlikely to ever see the dark-haired poetess again as long as he lived. That would, indeed, be for the better.

Still, he could not quite quiet the hope in him, which was blind, and stubborn as a songbird.

But, of course, the woman standing in the doorway was his step-mother.

'I received this letter today', Abigail Winters said, holding a simple folded sheet of paper aloft. 'Miss Deacon has left our company most surprisingly'. As she spoke these words, however, her eyes, usually merry, were burrowing tunnels through Edmund's forehead.

'We have had a disagreement'.

'Have you? May I ask about what? Pray tell me you did not argue about Homeric influences in Virgil'.

'There isn't much to argue about. Now that I've read the latter, I agree with her that there is little in Virgil but Homeric influences'.

'Such jesting is most unlike you'.

'This is a private matter, Mother'.

'I would hardly be a good mother if I left my son to stew in his own grievances. Please, Edmund, tell me." She walked over to him, and was now standing by the desk. 'What happened to her?'

'I have learned some things that made my courtship of her, let alone my marriage to her, impossible'.

He expected his stepmother to be shocked by the fact that such things were thought possible in the first place. Instead, she merely nodded.

'I thought you would be rather surprised', Edmund added.

'I would have been surprised had I not lived under the same roof as you. I might have been surprised had I not been present at that ball. But, as it is, the only thing that surprises me is that you thought me such a ninnyhammer as to miss these things. What were these things, besides the obvious matter of Miss Deacon's position? Has she murdered someone in the past?'

'Mother!'

'I am merely offering a version of events'.

'She had been...taken advantage of by... Well, I can scarcely call him a gentleman'.

'Good heavens'.

'Good heavens indeed. That...sordid liaison, though she did not want it, continued for years, with her mother's abetting'.

'But you said she did not want it.'

'She did not. But that is not the interpretation most people are going to settle on'.

'They might never know'.

'Affairs, they... They leave traces, like trails of wild beasts. I have found one. Someone might find another, or even stumble upon the same. Mother, I hope you realize— This is all for our family's sake. I would help her, of course I would, but how can I marry her?'

'But you want to'.

'It does not matter what I want. It never did'.

'This is the direst sentence I have ever encountered, and I have read most of Ann Radcliffe's novels'.

'If I do, it might mean our ruin. I know you have enjoyed Miss Deacon's company, but—'

'They won't take our money away." Abigail shrugged.

'I mean the ruination of our position in the eyes of the world'.

'Since when do you care about the world? You have fought most valiantly against even receiving guests'.

'I care about my father's legacy'.

There was an excruciating pause.

'Do you know', his stepmother finally said, breaking the silence like a wall of glass, 'some country on the Continent, I cannot quite recall which one, has this expression about trying to be holier than the pope in Rome'.

'I have never been particularly pious, Mother'.

'I think you understand it is merely an expression. Your pope is your father, has always been, and your particular piety is your notions of how the world ought to work'.

'The notions most gentlemen of sense, including him, share'.

'Edmund, how do you suppose my family took the news of his courting me all those years ago?'

'Excuse me?'

'Before I married your father and became the second Mrs. Winters. How do you suppose my family reacted to the notion of a man who made his fortune in trade intending to marry their blue-blooded daughter?'

'Not without consternation, I suppose'. The thought had only come into his head right now. It was peculiar, but, although he used to bristle at the notion of his father remarrying, he had grudgingly approved his choice of a bride—an earl's daughter, no less. Edmund had never thought to look at the situation from the other side of the looking glass, as it were, and ask himself how did the earl in question react to his daughter becoming a plain Mrs. Winters.

To some extent, he was excused by the fact that the marriage took place while he, Edmund, was at Oxford. When he came home to Morwood Hall for good, it was to a settled routine of a fashionable married couple, not to the drama of a courtship.

But only to some extent.

At this, his stepmother laughed, her laughter soft and silver.

'Not without consternation! You do have your father's gift for understatement, Edmund. My parents had been aghast. Now, had I been as rule-bound as you, I would have doubtlessly complied with their wishes and married a peer of their choosing. As it was, however, I persisted in my obstinacy until your father's proposal was finally, grudgingly, approved by mine. Your father did not live for long, after, to my great sorrow, but in the years we were married, I had been as happy as a woman can be'.

'That was rather different. If I marry Miss Deacon— God above, Mother, do you realize what it is going to mean for our standing? It is not only me who would become a laughingstock of the county. It is you, too'.

That was an old argument, a tired argument, one that had been running through his brain since the night of the ball. So tired it was, so close to being discarded, that bringing it out now seemed almost disingenuous. Still, Edmund supposed, it was an argument that his stepmother would understand better than any other.

'I know that. I would have lied if I said that I liked the prospect. But, to be frank, I like the concept of sharing house and home with your miserable countenance for the rest of my existence even less. God knows', she added impishly, 'you are not an easy man to live with even when your soul is in the state of perfect equanimity'.

'What if the word of her past gets out?' Edmund said, feeling curiously helpless, as though he was a shipwrecked traveler clutching on to a raft.

'Then make sure it does not. If you would be Miss Deacon's husband, it would be your duty to protect her, would it not? Is it not the duty of any husband?'

'Of course. I would never neglect my duty, whoever my wife may be'.

'What do you suppose is the point of this duty if it is never tested? How many women in our circle truly need some great protection from something in their lives? But she does. So give it to her'.

'I am. I will free her from the scoundrel's grasp if it shall be the last thing I do. But—'

'Do you love her, Edmund?' his stepmother asked bluntly.

'I do', he replied after a pause. Two words, but momentous, to his own ears, like a sigh from a stone.

'Then marry her. Do you suppose I was blind during the summer ball? You didn't speak like an automaton of the sort some German courts are fond of then. You spoke like a human being in love. You have snubbed the most eligible bride in Somerset for her. A man who only pursues his dreams halfway and stops before the first obstacle is not called a soul of propriety, he is a called a coward. I might be the silly, flighty creature you think me to be, but I know this. You have to go after her. Or one day some lady would take your hand and find out that your flesh really has turned to cold ivory'.

Chapter 15

F elicity did not leave her room for a long time.

She knew it would be only for the better.

Every knock on the door roused ghosts of ruin in her head. That unwanted rapping on wood must have been some worried friend—or gloating enemy—come with a scandal sheet to inform her of her downfall.

Felicity imagined her mother's expression change when the inevitable news came, and the vision elicited in equal parts thrill and fear in her. Was it likely to end badly for Felicity herself? Certainly. But so would a fire in this house that killed both of them, and it was not as though Felicity was not fantasizing about such a disaster now.

Whomever it was there, beyond the threshold, he or she refused to go away. Their knuckles must have been bleeding by now.

Felicity swallowed. There was no point in postponing the catastrophe.

She called for the maid to open the door.

A shuffle of footsteps, a breath of autumn. Summer was well and truly over now.

'Miss Deacon', the maid called out. 'There's a gentleman to see you!'

Felicity's heart skipped a beat. It could not be Anthony Flyte, could it? God in Heaven above, please, let it not be Anthony Flyte. There were challenges—quite a lot of challenges, latel–y—she did not feel herself equal to.

Felicity went into the small parlor, and froze.

'Edmund?' she asked, forgetting herself, forgetting the proper address they had returned to in that sun-dappled clearing. 'What are you doing here?'

Had she had any self-control left, she would have asked something more oblique. For example, if he is in London for long.

But she had none of it left. In truth, she had had very little left of anything.

'Felicity'. He did not bother to sit, and stepped toward her as soon as their eyes met. 'I have come to make things right'.

'What do you—'

Felicity did not finish the sentence when Edmund Winters grasped her hands in his. She heard the maid's shocked indrawn breath behind her, and footsteps from the corridor, but could not bear to pay attention to either.

'Felicity Deacon', the master of Morwood Hall whispered, looking in her face as though it were the sun, and he the reckless Icarus. 'Will you make me the happiest man on God's green earth by becoming my wife?'

'Do you truly mean this?'

'Of course'.

'But nothing has changed. I am still a danger to your standing.'

'Among whom? Among people like the Cadogans? God, but that would be a meager loss'.

'I am penniless'.

'No longer. Mr. Flyte chose a partial ruin over the greater one'.

'What do you mean?'

Edmund's face shone like a boy's, as though they were children again, fresh from some imagined victory over a great dragon.

'He has agreed to pay you what is owed to you. He would have agreed to far more, to be honest, just to avoid debtors' prison. I've checked the accounts after my steward did, and it seems you are quite a wealthy woman now, Felicity. Your dowry is nothing to be sneered at. I've promised to protect you, haven't I?'

'Yes, you have. I didn't believe you would. I didn't believe anyone would'.

'I would. I would, for the remainder of our lives, if only you—'

'Of course she agrees!' Mary Deacon exclaimed, standing in the doorway.

'Mother', Felicity muttered. 'Please, don't.'

'Of course she does', the older woman repeated, her smile bright and her gaze directed at her daughter vicious. 'She is not a fool, after all'.

'Mrs. Deacon', Edmund said coldly. 'It has been a long time since I saw you last'.

'You have changed so much'.

'And you not at all. I know about your—enterprise, Mrs. Deacon'.

'I cannot imagine what you mean'.

'I think you can. I would also tell you one thing. I could have said that, if your daughter accepts me, I would try to be a better protector to her than you were, but that would be setting the bar shamefully low'.

'Mr. Winters!' Mary Deacon's cheeks flamed with indignation under the fine powder. 'I don't know what Felicity told you, but I have always held her well-being close to my heart.'

'You have always held your own well-being close to your heart'.

Felicity's chest flooded with warmth—and not a little glee as she heard her mother's feeble protests. If Anthony Flyte was her dragon, her mother had been its servant and go-between. And now the man she had loved since she was but an adolescent had vanquished them both.

'Felicity!' Mary Deacon demanded. 'You cannot possibly be standing here, silent as a mule, and say nothing against such a treatment of me!'

'Oh, you are right. I cannot, and will not. I will say something indeed'. Felicity gave her a smile as cold as her own, an unsettling sharp mirror. 'I will not marry Edmund Winters in order to give you a route to the splendid life you have always thought yours by right. I will marry Edmund Winters because I love him, because he is a man of great decency and noble intentions. You are not going to be welcome in Morwood Hall, or indeed at our wedding. I will leave you the effects in this house, and a modest pension that would keep you from the rookeries. You have sold me like a harem-girl to keep yourself in good stockings. I think it would be fitting if now you will live knowing you do not starve on the street only because I will it'.

For a second, Felicity wondered if she had gone too far. If such a display of a vengeful nature would make Edmund reconsider his great proposal. But instead, she felt his hands press hers closer.

Felicity turned back to Edmund, and smiled.

'I will marry you', she repeated. 'I hope it will indeed make you the happiest man in the world. If not, I would have done something amiss. Should the mantua-makers of Bath and London be too scandalized by me', she added, 'I know a wonderful woman in the village closest to Morwood Hall who would do our wedding justice'.

Epilogue

F elicity Winters was slightly out of breath as she climbed over a hill.

'I would never understand how you manage to walk this valley so easily', she breathed, looking at her husband, who was waiting for her on the top. He offered her his hand, palm up, and she gratefully grasped it, as tightly as though she were a drowning woman.

But she was not drowning. Not anymore.

'It is mostly a matter of habit', Edmund told her. The sun was bright upon his face. Felicity could predict that only his forehead, shadowed by the hat, was going to remain white by this new summer's end.

'Then let us hope I am going to earn this habit soon enough'.

'I know you will. You train yourself into everything you put your mind to. You always have. Energetic rambling should not be harder than all those other matters'.

'It is certainly easier than household ledgers. I cannot understand how ladies born and bred manage to run such estates'.

'By being born and bred to them, mostly', Edmund replied. They were now strolling over thin, pale paths through the unclaimed grass.

'I hope your steward is skillful indeed, for I would not want Morwood Hall to go to ruin by the time our future children come of age'.

'The steward is skillful', Edmund put one hand upon her waist and turned her to face him, 'and the wife is clever'. With these words, he kissed her soundly.

For a few seconds, the world was gloriously still, frozen like a butterfly in amber. Then, Felicity laughed.

'Do be careful. What if someone spies us? It then shall be known that Mr. Winters is now consumed by a scandalous passion for his own wife'.

'It would hardly be more scandalous than our marriage'. With these words, he pressed his lips to the corner of her mouth.

Some kind of guilt twinged in her heart.

'I dearly hope you won't regret the fact'.

'Why would I, God above? I can live without invitations to hunt balls'.

Felicity thought back to their winter wedding—the world virginal in white, herself in a modest gown of blue muslin. While they walked back from the church, Felicity stepped very carefully along the paths, as though a careless touch that could break the surface of the snow could break her fragile future, too.

But nothing of the kind happened. The small procession reached the house without further adventures. The wedding breakfast was a quiet affair, lacking crowds from both his side and hers.

To be fair, Felicity and Edmund both were rather glad of it.

It had been tacitly agreed between them that, if she were now to pay for the expense of her publications—and, as Mrs. Winters, she could now well afford t-o—it would lend her the independence of creating she craved and was deprived of for so many years, and for such a great price. Privately, Felicity suspected she would recoup the investment well enough, for, if scandal closed some doors in the upper echelons of society, it made other things sell like hot cakes at Bartholomew Fair.

She did not write throughout this winter. The wound that gaped within her still needed time to mend, even now that the venom had been drawn out. She was sleeping, healing, walking with her husband arm in arm through the great white silence of the countryside day after day.

Something shifted in the spring, if not quite on the very same morning when Felicity jumped out of bed, ran to the window, opened it herself as though she lived in a farmer's cottage, and laughed at the April sunshine that soaked her top to toes. The air was tinted with lilies-of-the-valley.

'I am trying to write something new', Felicity said now, and swallowed as the last word left her lips. 'Well...something, at least. Anything at all'.

'Tell me'.

'It is going to be...something like the Roman pastorals, in a manner of speaking. Not that I am comparing myself to Virgil or my scribblings to his Georgics, but...' She halted, and had to find her bearing again. But find it she did. 'Do you remember I told you about *Abgrund*? The great chasm?'

'It's hard to forget, given the circumstances'.

'Yes, I suppose. Well, I... I am writing something that might be a farewell kiss to all those great chasms. An ode to these hills, to these woods, to that one chapel despoiled in King Henry's day."

'We shouldn't have visited it in March. Its beauty is far greater in summer'.

'I think, it was rather...right, in March. The cold light, the stained-glass, the jagged walls. It might not be as sweetly beautiful as a flower is beautiful, but it is something sublime'.

Felicity fell silent as Edmund touched her lower lip, stroking it wonderingly with his thumb.

'Something once abandoned and broken, but sublime? Isn't it rather prideful to be writing an ode to yourself?' he teased her, and her cheeks lit with heat that had nothing to do with the sunlight.

'It is not an ode to myself. Or at least I did not plan it this way. It is going to be an opening poem in a collection about this place'. Felicity stroked the nape of his neck, unable to resist the temptation of slight tickling, despite the earnest subject at hand. 'Or, rather, about our home'.

***

Did you enjoy this story? If so, perhaps, you would be interested in the next installment in the series, *A Novelist and an Earl*.

9 783982 550046